Finding Home: A Christmas Sweet Romance

Alice Fox

Published by Alice Fox, 2024.

This is a work of fiction. Similarities to real people, places, or events are entirely coincidental.

FINDING HOME: A CHRISTMAS SWEET ROMANCE

First edition. November 13, 2024.

ISBN: 979-8230924845

Written by Alice Fox.

Also by Alice Fox

More Than Roommates: An Enemies To Lovers Romance
His Bossy Obsession: A Billionaire Boss Romance
The Boss's Big Secret: A Billionaire Boss Romance
Falling for the Bosshole: A Billionaire Boss Office Romance
Taming the Bosshole: A Billionaire Boss Office Romance
Last Flight To Stardom: Enemies to Lovers Romance
Love In Full Bloom: Small Town Romance
Raindrops Over Texas: Small Town Cowboy Romance
Say Yes To The Boss: A Billionaire Boss Office Romance
Crushin' on Fame: A Billionaire Boss Romance
Dirty, Rich, Boss: A Billionaire Boss Office Romance
Queen of Hearts: A Dark Mafia Romance
Lost & Found: Small Town Romance
How Not to Fall For The Boss: A Billionaire Boss Romance
Irresistibly Bossy Collection: A Billionaire Boss Romance Collection, 3 Books In One
Behind Office Doors: A Billionaire Boss Romance
Finding Home: A Christmas Sweet Romance

Table of Contents

Charlotte Sweet found herself between a rock and a hard place when she aged out of the foster system. With only a car to her name, she set out on the open road, hoping to find long lost relatives. Winter hits her hard.

When she meets Cole Blackwood she's out of options but then he offers her a place to stay. As Christmas nears, she is given the chance at a normal life, but some chances come around too late. Will Lottie find the family she is looking for or head back out on the open road?

CHAPTER 1

Cole Blackwood

The wind whipped across my face as I opened the door of my truck. The winter air bit at my cheeks as my eyes watered from the impact. I pulled my hood up over my ears and pinched the front of my jacket closed as I made the short trip from my truck to the shop.

The bell dinged as I made my way through the customer entrance of the shop.

"What are you doing using the customer door, Eli?" Joe was acting every bit the boss he was.

"Well, Mr. Parker," I used his proper title, "in case you haven't noticed, it's eighty degrees below ice cold out there so I ran for the closest door."

"Well, get yourself ready to work, we already have three cars waiting for us." I walked toward the shop office as he continued, "First one's just an oil change and tire rotation, so you can take that on your own."

After I took off my jacket and turned up the shop radio, I made my way to the car Joe had pointed out to me and began the oil change by draining the old oil.

My day danced along with the songs on the shop radio as I tended to the tire rotations, oil changes, basic diagnostics, and other fascinating mechanical issues. Despite the speed with which we were working, there was still a backlog when lunch rolled around.

"Take your break, Eli." Joe was barely audible from his place underneath the Chevy he was working on. "I don't need your mother coming down here to speak with me about your nutrition again."

I couldn't help but laugh at his joke. "It's amazing to me that you're more worried about her than you are about the law," I stressed the last word as I finished washing my hands. "I mean, she's just my mom. What's she going to do to you?"

"Give me an earful and waste six hours of my time, if the last time is any indication." Joe rolled out from under the car and sat up before finishing his thought. "And . . . I actually think people work better when they are fed." He stood up and washed his hands as I stepped back to give him room. "So we are both going to get something to eat."

I bundled inside my jacket and gloves once more before opening the door and racing to my car. It wasn't until I had the door shut that I realized I hadn't remembered my wallet, which sat atop the desk in the shop office, mocking me.

There was no way I was braving that weather for an extra time, so there was only one thing to be done. I was going to visit my Mom.

I put the truck into first gear and pulled out of the parking spot my truck had shared with a snowbank for the last four hours. The streets were nearly empty as I took the four block trip to my family home.

"Mom!" I called as I stomped the snow off of my boots in the foyer. "I forgot my wallet at work so I'm going to borrow some lunch, okay?"

I didn't hear anything, so I took off my boots, gloves, and jacket and set them on the bench near the door. A small breeze nipped at my heel after sneaking in the crack at the base of the door.

"Hello, Cole," my Mom smiled as she slid a knife through the sandwich, "I made you ham, I hope that's all right."

"I can't believe you even heard me," I took a big bite of the sandwich she handed me, "I didn't think anyone was home."

"Manners, Cole, please!" She rolled her eyes at me.

I covered my mouth and mumbled a sorry before she continued.

"Your brother and sister are out with your dad getting a movie or a game or something for one of the grand babies." She put a glass of water down in front of me, "so it's just you and me for now. Will you be coming over for supper?"

Leave it to my mother to ask if I was coming for supper. "Seeing me once today isn't enough? I wasn't supposed to come over at all." I made sure my mouth wasn't full before answering this time. I guess Joe had a point about my mother.

"It is better than nothing," she smiled at me, "but not as good as twice."

"Well, I'll have to see. We're pretty busy at the shop today so I might stay late and just head home when I'm done work." I was giving myself an out, and she knew it.

"Okay, I was just hoping your brother and sister could see you, too." She got up to clean the already clean kitchen, "You are all so rarely in the same place. They miss you, you know?"

That woman really knew how to lay on the guilt trip. "I'll come over as soon as I can, Mom." I took my dishes to the sink, "I promise."

I was still finishing the second half of my sandwich when she finished the dishes. "You are welcome anytime. You know that."

I gave her a hug after stuffing the last bit of food into my mouth, "Thank you. I know, but I really have to go." Technically, that wasn't quite true as Joe gave me as much time as I wanted for lunch. But I wanted to get my apprenticeship hours completed, so I wanted to work as many of them as possible.

I ran back to my truck and was back working before Joe walked back into the shop. "Why are you using the customer entrance, Joe?" I'm pretty sure he threw a rag at me before cranking the radio up and getting to work.

❄❄❄

Six hours later, Joe and I had cleared all but two of the cars in the shop. "Lock up when you leave," Joe reminded me as he exited the building.

"Will do," I was just closing up the garage doors and turning out the lights and then I would be home free, "I'll see you tomorrow." We waved as he left and I locked the back entrance behind him.

If it's possible, by the time I left the garage, the wind was even colder. It pierced through the zipper of my jacket and chilled me to the core. I shivered involuntarily as I jogged across the street to get to my truck. My numb hands fumbled with the keys until I finally got the door unlocked and hopped inside.

The shell of the truck gave me some shelter from the wind, but it was still freezing inside as I turned on the ignition and cranked up the heat. Five minutes passed before the feeling returned to my fingers and I was able to adjust the radio dial to pick up the local overnight station. Ten more minutes passed before my truck windows were clear enough to drive. I silently cursed the winter as I put the truck in gear and pulled into the main roadway.

It was only seven o'clock the whole town rested as I drove home. The only thing open was the gas station and convenience store. As I passed, I honked the horn in two short bursts and raised my hand in greeting. It looked like Emmet behind the counter, but I couldn't be sure from this distance.

Three blocks later, and only two blocks from home, I noticed a car sitting in a snowbank. It was parked in the darkness between the light cast by the two nearest streetlights, so I had to pull up behind it to get a good look. It looked like whoever owned the car was having some difficulty because there was no logical reason for a car to be parked there at this hour.

I braved the cold to check if someone was inside needing help. I left the truck running so the lights would illuminate the car. As I passed the car, I could only get a glimpse through the window because they were covered with those shades meant to block out the sun. I knocked on the driver's window, and to my surprise, the car door opened to reveal a small, shivering woman.

"What do you want?" The driver looked afraid of me. I tried to peer inside, but she used her body to block me from seeing anything.

"Umm . . . hi, I'm Eli," I put out my gloved hand for her to shake. She looked at it and then back at me, so I continued. "I am a mechanic and I wondered if you might be having some car trouble."

Her nerves didn't seem to disappear, but her shoulders relaxed a little as she sat back into the driver's seat and rubbed her hands together to warm them. "I can't seem to get the heat to turn on any higher than this," she reluctantly moved aside so I could use my hand to feel the air coming out of the vent. "It's turned on high and it's still doing that. It's getting really cold in here."

"It's a little late now," I noticed a lot of things that normally weren't in cars, like plates and shampoo, lying on the front seat. "I can take you wherever you were going and have your car taken to the shop in the morning. I'm sure I can fix it up for you in no time at all."

She moved to get some things off the floor in the backseat and I noticed a sleeping back spread across the bench. Was she sleeping in this car? It didn't feel polite to ask, so instead, I just waited for her to collect her things and then walked her back to my truck.

"So," I asked as we closed the doors, "where do you want me to take you?"

She looked around, as though trying to find a place I could take her, before responding. "I don't really have anywhere to go. I was planning to just pass through town. Is there a hotel or something?" The way she squirmed made me wonder what was actually going on. Was she running from someone? I didn't know exactly what was going on, but I knew I had to help her and make sure she got somewhere safe. I could never forgive myself if something happened to her because I didn't help. Still, I wasn't exactly sure how to help.

"Uhh . . ." I cranked up the heat as I thought of what to say, "there's no hotel in town and the little bed-and-breakfast is closed for the winter so I don't think there's much by way of accommodations." I wasn't even sure how to approach the next topic, so I bit the bullet and went at it head on. "You could stay at my apartment if you want."

CHAPTER 2

Charlotte Sweet

My teeth chattered as my frozen fingers reached to adjust the heat. To say it was cold would have been an understatement. After an hour of trying to stay bundled and conserve my gas, I gave in. Freezing to death was becoming a real fear. The car's engine grumbled a low awful noise and I winced, if it broke down I wouldn't be able to afford to fix it and I had nowhere else to go.

I pressed my hands up against the vents, waiting impatiently for heat to pour out. "Come on," I muttered like my words would make the heat come faster. I sighed and my hands fell into my lap. It wasn't working. "Dammit!"

A knock at my window made me jump back. Standing in front of me was a young man, his hands held up as if to say he didn't want to hurt me. I stared forward and clenched my eyes shut. *Maybe if I ignore him he'll go away.* I crossed my fingers against my knees. Instead of walking back to his truck he knocked again.

I gulped. *Just make him leave and then move on from this town.* People were so annoying, butting into my business and running their mouths off. I bit my lip and hesitantly opened the door, the chilly breeze hitting my limbs. I could see my breath as I tried to calm my thoughts.

My feet were planted in the snow as I turned my body to face him. "What do you want?" My voice shook as I spoke, taking away the harshness of my tone.

"Umm . . . hi, I'm Eli," he thrust his hand towards me, introducing himself. All I could do was stare. *Wow, friendly.* It was evident that I was in a small town. His willingness to help was uncanny. "I am a mechanic and I wondered if you might be having some car trouble."

The cold made my hands shrivel up and curl into my flimsy jacket. The cold ate away at the walls I had put up and made me contemplate asking him for help. I couldn't live like this for long. The universe was holding out an olive branch, screaming at me that this was my one chance. Although there was a little voice in the back of my mind that said he was going to turn out to be an ax murderer.

"I can't seem to get the heat to turn on any higher than this," the words rolled off my tongue before I could think about what I was saying. He reached forward and pressed his hand against the vent. "It's turned on high and it's still doing that. It's getting really cold in here."

His eyes flickered to my backseat, where my whole life was displayed. I just hoped that my situation wasn't obvious from the food wrappers, hotel shampoo bottles, and open sleeping bag.

"It's a little late now, I can take you wherever you were going and have your car taken to the shop in the morning. I'm sure I can fix it up for you in no time at all." He offered. I nodded and reached into the backseat, throwing everything I could into my backpack. My clean clothes, the money I had saved up and the information that my social worker gave me on my family. Everything else was just stuff.

Eli guided me to his truck. "So where do you want me to take you?"

I froze as my hair plastered against my face. I didn't have a destination in mind, I barely even knew what town I was in. "I don't really have anywhere to go. I was planning to just pass through town. Is there a hotel or something?"

His eyes searched mine, as if he was waiting for me to tell him I was only joking. Eli quickly looked away and fiddled with his keys as he started the engine. Immediately the heat began to blast from the vents. My whole body relaxed as it devoured the warmth.

"Uhh, there's no hotel in town and the little bed and breakfast is closed for the winter so I don't think there's much by way of accommodations." His eyes met mine as he rambled as he searched for a solution like he could fix my problems. "You could stay at my apartment if you want."

I blinked, thinking I'd misheard him. He couldn't have just offered me somewhere to stay without asking anything in return or without ulterior motive. "What?"

"You can stay with me if you want, just until your car is fixed." He repeated himself. I had yet to find a strand of dishonesty in his eyes, but the fear lingered in my heart.

He had to want something in exchange, money, sex. There had to be something. "What's the catch?"

Hurt flashed across his face, but he was quick to shake it off. "No catch, just offering you a place to stay."

I wanted to run and I had every reason to. He was a stranger. I didn't know his intentions or his history. But it wasn't like I had another option, the warmth was making my decision for me.

"Okay," I mumbled. "Thank you."

My thoughts drifted as he drove, watching the windshield wipers rapidly push the falling snow away. I watched Eli out of the corner of my eye. He was intensely watching the road, but every few minutes he would glance in my direction like there was something he wanted to say. Each time he chickened out until he pulled into a driveway of a house with green gables. His body shifted towards me as he put the truck in park.

"I uh- I realized, I don't know your name."

I gulped. There was something so scary about telling him my name. It was like I was letting him in but what other choice did I have? "It's Lottie."

"Well it's nice to meet you, Lottie." He smiled as we fell into silence. Neither of us knew what to say next. We were strangers thrown into each others company. He cleared his throat, knocking his hands against the steering wheel. "Should we go inside?"

"Sure." I nodded, running my hands along my jeans. My heart lurched as I followed him to the front door. *Is this where he murders me?* I couldn't help but think the worst, but if it did work out then I would have somewhere safe to sleep tonight.

Eli fiddled with his key in the door and then held it open for me. "I just live down in the basement apartment. Mr. and Mrs. Wilson let me stay in the basement for a good price. The salary of a mechanic isn't the best so anything helps." He trailed off and I felt myself relax. The knowledge that there would be someone else staying a floor up put me at ease. "Sorry I ramble when I'm nervous."

"It's okay," I mumbled and stepped inside. It was like a blanket of warmth washed over me.

Eli closed the door behind me and led me down to his apartment. It was cozy, with a small kitchen and living room that butt up against each other.

He headed towards a closed door. "This is the bedroom, you can have the bed tonight." I opened my mouth to tell him I could sleep on the couch but he cut me off. "I insist. You should get a good night's sleep." He turned to the left. "This is the bathroom, feel free to take a shower or whatever." He reached into the cupboard and pulled out a green towel and face cloth. "I'll be out here if you need anything else."

I nodded. It seemed to be my signature response. My body ached for a hot shower but I couldn't help myself from watching as he walked into the kitchen. There was something intriguing about him. The selfless way he took in a stranger. The sparkle behind his deep brown eyes.

His eyes met mine and I quickly looked away, retreating into the washroom. I let the water run, waiting for it to warm up before getting into the shower.

As the water cascaded down my body, it took away the chill. I wasn't sure how long I stood there for, before I got out, wrapping the towel around myself.

I caught a glimpse of myself in the mirror. The girl I saw was unrecognizable, with hollow cheeks and heavy bags under her eyes. It took me a minute to realize I was looking at my reflection and not a stranger. I rummaged through my bag, searching for a pair of pajamas. Buried at the bottom was a tattered pair of cat pajamas.

As I stepped out of the bathroom a delicious smell hit my nose. Eli's head shot up, as if he was waiting for me. In front of him were two plates piled with food, I assumed one for me and one for him.

"I thought you might be hungry. I know I am. I made a stirfry." He pushed a plate towards me and motioned for me to sit down. Right on cue my stomach growled. "Guess I was right," he chuckled to himself.

"Thank you." The chair legs screeched against the floor and I sat down.

"So uh- what brings you to Willowtree Valley?" He asked just as I took my first bite.

"Like I said, I was just passing through. On my way to visit family." I kept it brief, hoping he would be satisfied with my answer. I wasn't in the mood to get into the details and I didn't want to burden him with the reality of things.

"Sorry, I didn't mean to pry," he quickly apologized.

I sighed. Maybe I was too harsh or rude. "It's okay."

We continued to eat in silence, until my fork scraped the bottom. "I can take your plate." He scooped up the plate and laid it in the sink.

"Thanks, it was really good," I muttered as I got up and pushed my chair back in. "Goodnight."

"Goodnight Lottie." He smiled.

I threw myself into the covers and fell asleep as soon as my head hit the pillow.

CHAPTER 3

Cole Blackwood

When I peeled my eyes open in the morning, it took me a few seconds to remember why I was lying on my couch instead of in my bed. Lottie. I don't know what came over me to ask her to stay but I was glad I had; it was cold inside my apartment, so I didn't want to imagine how cold it was outside. I heard movement in the kitchen and wondered if Mr. Wilson had come down to try to fix the leaky tap again. I kept telling him we should just hire someone to do it but he kept trying to fix it himself.

"Hi. Sorry I woke you." It was Lottie. I sat up on the couch to look over at her standing in the kitchen.

"Good morning. You didn't wake me. Did you sleep all right?"

"Yeah, your bed was surprisingly comfortable," it was possible she was blushing a little. I wondered why, but didn't think we knew each other well enough that I could ask her.

"Good. I'm glad." I smiled as she ducked her head down to pick something up off the floor. "Do you need some help?"

"Oh, uh, no! I'm fine, I just. . ." she sighed, "I do need help. I was trying to do the dishes, but I can't find your soap."

"You don't have to do that," I stood up to go help her, the blanket falling to my feet as I did so, "you're the guest."

I rounded the edge of the counter into the kitchen and Lottie looked up at me. Her hair was covering part of her face, having fallen there as she searched the lower cabinets hoping to find the dish soap. She could have brushed it out of her eyes, but instead chose to hide behind it as she blushed.

"Uh, Eli?"

"Yeah?" I reached up to the top shelf and brought down the dish soap.

"You aren't wearing a shirt."

"Yeah, so?"

"You are not exactly wearing pants."

Instinctively, I covered myself with my hands. I looked down to see what she meant and let out a small laugh. It's just underwear! It's not like she saw anything.

"Sorry, I'll go put something more on," I was already halfway to my room because of the initial fear response.

I was surprised I even heard her from that distance as she muttered to herself, "I can't believe I just did that... so embarrassing... see my stuff."

I went into my dresser and found the only pair of pyjama pants I owned. I never slept in pyjamas unless I visited my parents, so they still looked like they were brand new, even after nearly three years of use. I should have worn them last night, but by the time I realized what was going on, Lottie was already in bed.

I turned around at the door and went back to put a shirt on, too, because it seemed like Lottie would be more comfortable that way.

I jogged back out to the kitchen to help Lottie with the dishes. "I told you that you didn't have to do the dishes, Lottie."

"And I told you I wanted to help you because you helped me." Her gaze was intense, so I let it drop.

"Okay, how about I dry?" I picked up the dish towel as a peace offering and she accepted.

"Fine, you can dry." She handed me the cup she had just finished washing.

"Speaking of helping you," I thought we might as well get right to the point about her car, "we have to get your car into the shop today. I wasn't supposed to work but Joe never minds when I put in some overtime."

She was focusing intently on the plate she was washing, and avoiding my gaze.

"Is it okay if we go together to get your car towed and you can get whatever else you need out of there? Once it's at the shop, you can hang out in the shops nearby or whatever until I figure out what's wrong with your car?"

I did not understand what was making her so quiet all of a sudden, so I decided the next shot would be my last for now, "Or I can go by myself if you want to give me the keys?"

"No!" She almost dropped the plate she was still washing, "I'll come, that sounds great. I do have some stuff I should probably get out of there anyway." *Wasn't that the truth?*

"Okay, sounds good. We can go after breakfast."

We continued to wash dishes in silence. Every time I looked over at her, I couldn't tell what she was thinking. Her face was mostly stoic and emotionless, but there was no way a girl with no one nearby would be emotionless about this situation, so she must have been good at hiding what she really felt.

As we finished up the dishes, I made some toast for Lottie and got myself a bowl of cereal with milk. We sat down and started eating, still in relative silence. I didn't know if it would be a good idea, but I was going to break the ice. Again.

"So, when we're done eating, I'll give the tow truck a call and tell him where to meet us and then we can drive over to where you left your car and wait for him." I pulled out my cell phone and looked up the number and then wrote it down in my phone's notes section.

"Yeah, okay." She looked down at her lap.

I looked over at Lottie's empty plate and wondered if there was something else I could get for her. This house really wasn't equipped for company. "Do you want something else? I have a bit of cereal left. I guess I need to go shopping."

She laughed a little at the silly face I made. "I guess so, yeah. I'll be fine until lunch. Thanks."

That was more words than I'd gotten out of her all morning since I had put on real clothes. "No problem." I took the dishes to the sink.

I was in the middle of drinking my glass of water when I realized I hadn't offered Lottie a phone to call her folks. Surely, if she was supposed to meet them, they'd be worried about her by now. I was definitely not the most considerate person in the universe.

"Lottie?" I called out, hoping she could hear me from the bedroom where she was getting dressed.

"Yeah?" She rounded the corner into the hallway as she spoke.

"I wondered if you might need to borrow a phone to call your folks. They must be worried about you."

Her face dropped a fraction before her neutral expression returned and then was replaced with a polite smile. "No one will worry. Plus, I have my own phone."

She had her own phone. Who didn't have their own phone nowadays? "Oh, right. Of course. So, are you ready to go?"

She nodded her head so I picked up my phone to call for the tow truck while we put on our coats and mitts. I grabbed my keys and followed Lottie out the door, locking it as we left.

❆❆❆

We arrived at Lottie's car before the tow truck, so she went to grab some of her things while I waited in the truck. I was staying in the truck because when I offered to help, the glare she gave me could have turned the snow banks into flames.

I sat in the truck and periodically checked to see if I could see a tow truck coming from either direction. Mostly, I just watched Lottie. I couldn't figure her out. One second she was being sweet and nice and making me feel like I should give her a hug, and the next she was shooting daggers at me with her eyes. In that particular second, she was stretching out on the back seat of her car trying to reach something far under the driver's seat. My instincts were telling me to go help her, but her warning earlier kept me firmly planted in my truck.

Five minutes later, Lottie returned with two bags of her things and put them into the back of the truck.

"Thanks for not coming over," she said as she returned to the cab of the truck, "I appreciate it."

Any other girl and I would have assumed that statement to be dripping with sarcasm, but something about Lottie made me believe she really was happy I had let her be and done as she asked.

"You're welcome!" I smiled at her a little too intently, "I am always happy to do nothing to help other people."

She laughed a little at my joke as she rubbed her hands together to warm them by the heater. "Can you turn it up a little? My hands are freezing!"

I reached over and turned the heat up just as I saw the tow truck round the corner in front of us. "You stay here and get warm," I moved to open my door, "I'll deal with them and we can follow it to the shop."

"Thank you" her voice was barely loud enough to hear over the truck's engine.

"Anytime," I smiled as I shut the door behind me and went to tell the tow truck driver what to do with Lottie's car.

When I had finished helping him hook her car up to his truck to speed up the process, I gave him the address to the shop. Apparently, he was very new to driving a tow truck in this area, because Joe's shop was the only one around. I turned back toward my truck and noticed Lottie dancing along to whatever music she had playing in the truck. From here, it looked like she was dancing to the sounds of the highway traffic going by and the kids playing with their grandparents in the house across the street.

She had a lot on her plate with a broken car in the middle of a road trip and no family to come to pick her up, but she still managed to have a little fun. I was so curious to see what song she was listening to that I almost jogged back to the truck, despite the ice and snow that covered the street. I was not disappointed.

CHAPTER 4

Charlotte Sweet

Eli looked like he knew what he was doing as he fiddled around. I, on the other hand, knew close to nothing about cars. I was sat off to the side, but close enough that I could watch him work. My hands were wrapped around a cup of tea, but it wasn't the warmth that turned my cheeks a bright shade of red. As he reached across the car his shirt lifted from his side, while the muscles in his back flexed. I would have to be blind not to notice how attractive he was.

He turned back to me, wiping the grease on his hands off on a rag and pulled up a chair. "Well the heat actually looks like an easy fix, but the alternator is what's concerning me. You wouldn't have made it much further. Unfortunately, I don't have any on hand so we'll have to order one for you but that shouldn't take too long."

"H-how much will that be?" I stuttered, my voice quiet. I reached into my bag and pulled out my wallet. My savings were dwindling quickly. From a quick glance, there were less than five hundred dollars left and I was still a ways away from my final destination. I gulped, feeling my heart sink into my stomach.

Eli reached forward and placed his hand on mine. My body froze at the unexpected human contact but quickly relaxed from the sincere look on his face. "It will be around four hundred, but you don't have to pay me now. The part won't be in for a few days at least."

"I don't know Eli," I sighed, shaking my head. I looked down, counting the bills in my head. Could I really afford it? I had no source of income, no way to pay him back for his kindness.

His phone vibrated against the workbench. He quickly jumped up, checking the caller ID. "Sorry, it's my mom, I'll just be a minute."

He paced the garage as he spoke to his mom, a big smile on his face the whole time. From what I heard they seemed to have a good relationship, the kind that I was longing for. Throughout high school, girls were constantly complaining about their mothers. Some were too overprotective, or too embarrassing. Sometimes I just wanted to yell at them to shut up. A mother was an important figure in a girls' life and I didn't have one.

Eli hung up and shoved his phone in his jeans pocket, lightly jogging back over to me. "My mom needs some help at the cafe, do you want to come with? It's not far from here. You don't have to if you don't want to..." He rubbed the back of his neck as if he was flustered.

"Yeah sure, I'll come." *What else do I have to do?* I bit my lip and put on my jacket. "What does your mom think of a strange girl staying with you?"

He chuckled lightly and shrugged. "She was surprised at first, but she said she would have done the same thing if she saw you on the

"Wow," I muttered, involuntarily. Generosity wasn't something I was used to. In my experience, all people cared about was money and power.

"What?" he asked, nudging my shoulder.

I chuckled, awkwardly. "Nothing, just the generosity, it blows me away. Guess I'm just not used to it."

His jaw hung unhinged, trying to process what I'd said. I caught him off guard, left him speechless. The reality of my life was too hard for some people to handle. That, I was used to.

"It's okay though, I know good people exist. Just haven't met many," I rambled on, trying to lighten the mood but it didn't seem to work. The shocked look on his face turned sympathetic.

"That sounds really tough. I can't imagine a world where I didn't trust anyone to give me a helping hand when I needed it. Probably wouldn't be here." He gave me a smile and opened a door for me. I stepped into a cafe, booming with business. Every seat was filled. It smelled heavenly, of pastries and chocolate, with a hint of peppermint and fir trees. It was what I imagined the perfect Christmas to smell like.

A woman strutted up to us, a big smile on her face and two aprons slung over her arm. She seemed full of joy, untouched from hardship. Although deep down I knew that wasn't the case, everyone knew pain she just made the best of the cards she had been dealt. She reached out for Eli and put her hands on his cheeks. "Oh Cole."

"Hi mom," Eli laughed.

It was like everything fell into place. I now knew where Eli got his warmth from. She turned to me and took my hands. "You must be Lottie, I'm Janae but everyone calls me Jan. I am so glad you both are here because I could really use your help." She slung the apron over my head and tucked a notebook in the pocket before either of us had a chance to object.

"Just tell me where you want me." Eli tied the apron behind his back like second nature and slid a pen behind his ear. "I can show Lottie the ropes."

"You're a lifesaver, both of you! Why don't you each take half the room, see if anyone is finished and take orders for new customers?" She smiled. A bell dinged and she quickly scurried off behind the cash register.

"Sorry, she can be a bit much for newcomers." Eli apologized.

I quickly shook my head. "She seems great, I like her. Do you do this often?" I asked, gesturing to the apron.

"Not in a while, but it was my part-time job as a teenager."

"Is it always this busy?" I wondered out loud.

"No, just during the holidays. Mom makes a special Christmas menu." He gestured for me to turn around. My eyes widened, making up silly reasons in my head for why he'd want me to do so. "I'll tie your apron."

"Oh," I mumbled, my cheeks turning a bright shade of red. I quickly spun around. His hands brushed against my back as he tied the strings around my waist and into a bow. "Thanks." I took a deep breath and looked around the room. "So what do I need to do."

"Anyone new who comes in you'll just take their order and write it down in the notebook, each table on a separate page. Then you'll relay it to my mom and she'll get the order ready. When she rings the bell that means the order is ready and she wants one of us to deliver it to the table. When you see someone get up you can clean the table off." I bit my lip, nervously. I was bound to forget something. Waitressing would be a new experience, one I wasn't sure I would be any good at. "Just follow my lead, you'll be fine."

"Okay." He squeezed my shoulder and headed towards a table, picking up two menus on the way. "Hi my name is Eli and I'll be your server today." He placed the menus down in front of the couple. "What can I get for you?"

I sighed, scanning the room. An older woman sat down at a table and laid her purse down on the chair next to her. I picked up a menu, repeating what Eli had said in my head. "Hi I'm Lottie, I'll be your server today. What can I get for you?"

I glanced over at Eli, my eyes meeting his. He gave me a thumbs up and smiled.

"Can I have a small coffee with milk and a shortbread cookie dear?"

❆❆❆

Jan locked the door, waving goodbye to the last trickling customers and turned off the open sign. My feet throbbed as I sat down in one of the chairs. "Thank you so much for your help today, I really appreciate it. Made the day go so much smoother. What I would give to have your help all the time."

Eli chuckled. "You know I have to work Mom."

"What about you Lottie? Would you be interested in helping me out for the holidays? I would pay you of course. We also get some very generous tippers in here." This time I was left speechless. Another kind gesture. I was beginning to think I was dreaming. She didn't know me or have any stake in my future. Just like that, she was offering me a job. A way to pay Eli for his generosity and work on my car.

"Uh, I would be happy to help. Thank you."

She shook her head. "No thank you, you did a great job today. You'd be doing me a favor. As you saw today, it's quite a busy time. I can use all the help I can get. Now, who's hungry?"

Smelling the sweets all day was torture. I was just dying to taste something.

"Oh yeah, I'm starving." Eli jumped out of his seat and rubbed his hands together. He headed towards the kitchen but his mom stopped him.

"Patience my boy." She showed him to the seat across from me. "I'll be right back."

Eli sighed and leaned across the table. I took a second to look around. Now that the cafe was empty I could see the appeal. It was cute and cozy, the kind of place full of family and love.

"All this food is made by your mom?" I asked.

"That's how it started out but now there are a few people who help out with the baking. Her recipes though." He explained. The smile on his face grew as he spoke of her, I could tell he was proud of her accomplishments.

"Wow, she's an amazing woman."

"What does your mother do?" He asked. It was an innocent question, but a loaded one. He had no idea what he was jumping into. My past was hard to explain. People liked to make assumptions about who I was because of my experiences. "Lottie?"

I shook the thoughts from my head. "Sorry, I uh- don't know actually. I've never met her."

Eli opened his mouth, but Jan burst through the kitchen door thankfully ending our conversation. She placed a bowl of pea soup in front of me and a slice of homemade bread, but my eyes were locked with Eli's. I had a feeling he had many more questions he wanted to ask me. Dread sat in the pit of my stomach.

Right now I was the mysterious girl on the side of the road. What would he think of me when he found out the truth?

CHAPTER 5

Cole Blackwood

I didn't know how to respond to Lottie's revelation that her mother had died, so I just ignored it. Generally, ignoring something like that is a bad idea. But when that someone is going to leave town in a week once you fix her car, exceptions can be made.

Lottie was chatting so much with my mom that neither one of them had touched their dinner when I finished mine, so I took the opportunity to head over to the shop and make sure everything was closed up since I had left in such a rush.

Or that's what I told them. I knew I had locked everything but I wanted some time to think about Lottie. She was still such a mystery and I wanted to know more but I didn't know how to ask. *Oh, hey, how's your dead mom?* Doesn't sound too nice. Maybe I could ask her about her dad? I used to make friends all the time, how was it possible that I couldn't figure out how to talk to her?

I stood outside the diner watching her chat with my mom, the two of them laughing at some private joke. I couldn't help but smile as I stood outside in the snow, forgetting all about the cold. I don't know how long I stood there, but I'm sure it was longer than a normal person would have, so I made my way inside and caught the tail end of a conversation I couldn't believe my mother was having with the girl I . . . The girl who was staying in my house.

❄❄❄

I threw my keys down onto the counter as we entered my apartment. Lottie's laugh filled the whole room as my face warmed from embarrassment.

"I can't believe she told you that," I buried my face in my hands to avoid looking at Lottie's eyes.

"I think your mom might be the best part of this whole 'stuck in this town' situation," Lottie continued to laugh as she walked towards the bedroom. "I can't believe you used to run naked down the middle of the street!"

"I was two!" I knew there was nothing I could say to make her stop laughing, but I felt the need to defend myself given this morning's near-miss on nakedness.

"And I can't believe no one has any pictures of it, because I want one!" she laughed from behind the bedroom door as I awaited her return. The heat in my face grew more intense.

"Oh, Mom never got to that part of the story?"

She popped her head into the doorway, "What part of the story?"

I smiled and raised my eyebrow, "The part where she caught me making a bonfire in our backyard."

Lottie's eyes widened and her mouth formed a small o shape, "You didn't!"

I just nodded, trying to keep my expression steady.

This time, when she laughed, I laughed with her. I was fixated on how beautiful her face was when she was truly happy. She looked up and caught me staring, so I broke my gaze briefly. I risked a glance towards her and noticed her cheeks were red; was I embarrassing her or was it possible she was looking at me the same way I was looking at her?

I sobered up a little when I realized I hadn't seen her smile very much since she arrived. I supposed that was normal after being stranded in a town where she knew no one, but it still made me wish there was something more I could do to make this easier for her.

"Hey, Lottie?" I called through the door she had once again closed in order to get changed, "You up for some video games or a movie or something?"

There was a brief pause before she came out in what looked like they were pajamas, "I don't know, are you ready to get your butt kicked?"

She rifled through my collection of ancient video games while I showered and found some suitable sleeping clothes to avoid a repeat of this morning. No need to embarrass myself more than usual.

"So, what are we playing?" I returned to the living room to see her laying across my armchair reading one of the many comic books I have lying about every surface in my apartment.

She jumped a little at the sound of my voice before putting the comic back on the table beside her, "I'm thinking we race." She smiled as she held up a Mario Kart game in front of her face like a fan.

We agreed on a best of seven and shook hands - loser does tomorrow's dishes. I tried not to let her see it, but talking to her about who would do what household chore tomorrow made me think about what it might be like if she stayed longer. I knew she would leave once her car was finished, of course, so I was quietly grateful that she would have to wait at least a week for the parts to come in. At least I would get to spend some time getting to know her. I smiled at the thought of having her here that long and looked over to see her attention fully on the screen. Only then did I realize we had begun the race that I would most definitely lose.

Due to my extremely poor showing, it only took her five races to win the best of seven. She cheered her triumph as she crossed the line in second place, only one spot ahead of me.

"I need a snack," I said as I put down my controller. "Do you want anything?"

She looked down at her lap and wrung her hands before she answered me, "Oh, I don't think I need anything." It seemed to me that she didn't want to impose, but I didn't want her to feel uncomfortable here. I suddenly remembered I had found her presumably living in her car only yesterday. How was it possible for me to forget something like that? I turned away from her so she wouldn't see the look on my face.

"I'm making nachos, then." I pulled myself together enough to continue a normal conversation, "Do you want to help me grate cheese?"

She sat at the counter while we worked. My brain was working overtime trying to find a topic of conversation. I wanted desperately to talk more about her revelation that she had never met her mother, but I could tell from the look on her face at the cafe that she was relieved to not have to speak about it. I wanted to know everything about her, but I couldn't risk driving her away.

"Are those chips training for the army?" Lottie's voice broke me out of my inner monologue.

"Uh . . . " I struggled to figure out what she was talking about, "Sorry, what?"

She shook her head and laughed as she popped a piece of cheese into her mouth before getting up to bring the bowl of cheese to where I was standing.

"I asked if the chips were training for the army. You seem to be putting them through training for several formations when really you just need to dump them onto the pan."

"Oh, uh . . ." My brain wasn't working with her standing so close to me, "Oh, no. I was just. . ."

She laughed again, "How about I do that?" She took the pan from my hands and started layering the toppings on the chips.

"So, where are you from?" My brain had finally come up with an innocuous topic to discuss, "Somewhere warm?"

She finished putting the cheese on the nachos. She started to speak and then stopped herself several times before she finally answered me, "I . . . Uh, what makes you say that?"

I was guessing that saying *you didn't seem prepared for the cold weather based on the clothes that were in your car* was out, so I tried to move around the subject. "Just optimistic, I guess. I always wanted to live somewhere warm."

"Well, it's not as cold as here, I guess." The chips were in the oven now so we were both intently staring through the door, watching the pile of cheese Lottie had used slowly melt.

"Well, I'm from right here. Born and raised," I smiled at her, though she did not look at me. "I did leave once for a little while."

She looked at me, then, her face seemed heavy.

"Why did you leave? Is this another story about how five-year-old Eli ran away from home?"

I silently cursed my mother for telling all those stories; she could be a lot sometimes. I shook my head, "No. This is another 'there's no trade school in this town' story. I had to leave town to go to school if I wanted to be a mechanic. I think my parents would have rather I learned to cook, but sometimes you have to step outside what your parents want for you, I guess."

Her eyes snapped back to the oven when I looked at her, so I couldn't gauge her reaction from her expression when she responded, "Yeah, I guess it happens to most people. It's good that you know what you want to do and found a way to do it, though."

I had never thought about it that way. My whole life I had known I could do what I wanted and that I would go to school to train for whatever I decided. My parents weren't super excited about my becoming a mechanic, but they weren't unsupportive either. It never occurred to me that other people might not live in a world where they got the schooling they needed to do the job they wanted. I was saved from any response by the bubbling cheese in the oven.

"Oven mitt! I need an oven mitt!" Lottie was scurrying about the kitchen in a futile attempt to find an oven mitt I did not own.

"Here, let me," I stepped in front of her and used a dish towel to pull the pan out of the oven and drop it onto the stovetop. I wasn't quite fast enough to avoid all damage, and I could feel the burn sliding up my fingers as I turned the cold water on and held my hands under the water.

Lottie looked at me, "Are you alright? I feel like this is why people have oven mitts." Her voice was a mixture of concern and mockery.

"I'll be okay," I shook the water off my hand and dried my hands, "those mechanic calluses come in handy sometimes."

She took my hand in both of hers and looked at the tips of my fingers. Her hands were remarkably soft and stood in stark contrast to my own in every way. I watched as a small piece of her hair fell in front of her face, and resisted the urge to brush it behind her ear; I wasn't sure if she would appreciate the gesture.

"It looks like it will be fine. I don't see any blisters," she seemed to know what she was doing.

"Thanks. Glad to hear it," I smiled and reluctantly took my hand from hers, "So let's eat these nachos before we get to our rematch, okay?"

❄❄❄

I couldn't believe she beat me again. When she won the fourth game, I officially gave up for the night.

"So, I don't know if this interests you, but my family have this kind of tradition," I waited to see how she would react before continuing, "Two weekends before Christmas, we all go together to cut down a tree and then we take it home and decorate it. Well, Mom wants me to come and she has invited you, but we don't have to go if you don't want to or don't feel comfortable or whatever." I was trying to give her an out, but she didn't take it.

"That sounds really nice," she smiled as her eyes seemed to stare into the distance, "I've always wanted to have a real Christmas tree."

I contorted my face a little, "They aren't all they're cracked up to be. A lot of cleaning up needles and watering and whatnot, but it's a tradition and we usually have cocoa and eat snacks and decorate the tree. It's pretty fun and, as you know, Mom's food is always top-notch."

"Sounds nice, I. . ." she seemed to catch herself mid-sentence. "I'd love to go."

"I'll tell her we'll be there," I smiled at her, "I know she'll be happy that you're there."

I would be happy, too.

CHAPTER 6

Charlotte Sweet

I pulled my mittens up over my wrists and hopped out of Eli's truck, my feet landing in the soft powdery snow. It was as if I had stepped into a world that only existed in dreams. The snow lying on the tree branches glistened as the warm white lights tried to peek through the daylight. Colors of red and green littered the farm, along with little wooden reindeer, creating the perfect scene of Christmas. Not to mention the intoxicating smell of evergreen trees that lit up my senses.

My smile was briefly replaced by a frown as my childhood dreams danced around in my mind. It was hard to imagine what life would have been like if I had been born into the perfect family, but I liked to think we would have gone to a place like this where magic was only just around the river bend. Tears pooled in my eyes, making the twinkling lights blur into stars.

"Are you alright dear?" Jan wrapped her arm around my back. I hadn't even noticed her and her husband pull up beside us.

The dreams quickly faded as I snapped back to reality. Blinking away the tears I nodded, my eyes locking with Eli's as he emerged around the corner straightening the Santa hat on top of his head.

"Let's find a tree. Shall we?" His voice was filled with excitement as he reached up, another Santa hat in his hand. Eli placed in on my head, bending down to make sure it was on straight. He tucked a loose strand of hair behind my ear before looking satisfied.

Eli's dad stepped forward and held out his hand. It seemed like a genuine gesture, despite his rough, messy appearance and large shadow that towered over me. "We haven't officially met yet, I'm Robert."

I shook his hand. "It's nice to meet you."

"Let's get this show on the road," Robert announced and started into the rows of trees.

"Why don't we split up? We'll cover more ground so we can find the perfect tree." Jan suggested, but I saw an ulterior motive in her eyes as she followed her husband. I even thought I saw her wink at Eli but I quickly shook my head of any thoughts of romance. There was no chance for us. He knew I was only going to be in town for a few days.

There were so many trees to pick from. Each one unique, like a snowflake. "So uh- how do we do this?"

"It's simple really if you see a tree you like let me know and we'll take it home." He turned to face me, walking down the aisle backward. I chuckled before I realized he was serious.

"What? It's your family tree, I can't-"

He cut me off. "Yes, you can." Eli waited for me to catch up, so we were walking side by side before taking me by the shoulders and pointing me in the direction of the trees. "They're calling you." He held his hands up to his mouth. "Lottie! Lottie! Pick me!"

I shook my head, laughing. "You're so weird."

"I'm going to take that as a compliment." He smiled. "My sister always loved picking out the Christmas tree. She called it the centerpiece of Christmas."

His use of past tense threw me off guard. Most would have probably assumed she was away at college or out seeing the world. My cynical brain immediately thought that she was dead. I gulped, treading lightly. "Where is your sister now?"

"She's lives not far from here actually. She's married with two kids, my niece, and nephew." He smiled brightly, his eyes lighting up as he spoke about them. It was inspiring and contagious. A smile pulled at my lips. It was the feeling I longed for my whole life, to have a love so big that it showed on my face. "They got their Christmas tree the other day, but they'll join us on Christmas Eve and Christmas day."

"It sounds like you have some really lovely family traditions," I said, putting my hands in my pockets as I felt the cold nip at my fingertips.

He nodded, shrugging his shoulders. "Yeah, I guess it's easy to take those kinds of things for granted. It's all I've known really, but I can't imagine it any other way."

We wandered further down the rows of trees, my arm brushing against the needles. His life seemed picturesque, yet he was kind and compassionate. He was unlike anyone I'd ever met. Within days, I felt closer to him than anyone I'd ever known and somehow, despite years of maltreatment and abandonment, I trusted him. It intrigued me, I wanted to know more about him and how he grew up. "Do you have any other siblings?"

"Yeah, I also have an older brother. He works shifts so he couldn't join us today, much to my mom's dismay. I swear she still thinks we're little kids, but it is nice when we get to do things together like old times. Guess that's kind of the spirit of Christmas." He chuckled, before stopping in his tracks. I watched as he reached towards a tree and stood it up straight. "What about this one?"

I looked it over, but there was something about it that didn't feel right. From the way Eli talked, I felt like I was supposed to get a feeling in the pit of my stomach and just know.

"No?" Eli knew immediately by my silence.

"No, not that one." I shook my head.

He smiled, looking pleased. "When you know, you know."

Eli abruptly turned a corner and headed down the next row. I jogged to catch up with him, my breath making small white puffs in the air.

"How about you?" He asked, breaking the silence. I furrowed my eyebrows, not quite sure what he was getting at. He quickly caught on. "Any siblings?"

I bit my lip, my teeth pulling at a dry patch of skin. I felt a pang in my chest when I thought about lying. He had been so kind, letting me into his home, letting me get to know him and his family. Yet he barely knew anything about me. I had a feeling that the intrigue of the mystery was going to get old fast. "I think I have a sister. At least that's what I've been told." *Please don't pry, please don't pry,* I begged. I got my wish, he didn't ask further but it could have been because he didn't get the chance. He just flashed me a sympathetic expression. "You know what I've always wanted to do?"

His body language quickly shifted as he chuckled. "What?"

"I've always wanted to go tobogganing. I keep seeing it in movies and it looks like so much fun." I told him and he beamed at me. The mischievous look in his eyes told me he was planning something, like an impromptu tobogganing trip. He kept his mouth shut though as if it was going to be a surprise when I was least expecting it. "Oh, and I want to make a snowman." I quickly added, winking.

I turned back to the trees, my eyes catching the perfect one. Eli was right, it was a feeling in the pit of my stomach. The way my heart clenched and my breathing halted momentarily. I'd found it, my first Christmas tree. Tears pooled, threatening to spill down my cheeks. The tree stood alone at the end of the aisle. Its branches were sparse and stuck out every which way. All of its mates had already been sold and gone home to nice warm houses. The story of the ugly duckling popped into my head and I remembered how much I felt like that was me. The last kid left in the group homes, the one who never got adopted. I wasn't about to let this tree have the same fate.

I gulped and picked up the shaggy tree, turning to Eli. "This is the one."

He laughed a throaty laugh before he realized that I wasn't joking. I was dead serious. "Oh..." He examined the tree, walking around it several times. "Okay." Eli picked it up and sighed. "Why this one, if you don't mind me asking?"

I hesitated, thinking about my answer. "I know what it's like to feel alone and no one deserves that, not even a tree."

This time when I looked at Eli I didn't quite understand the look in his eyes. It was new, sending shivers down my spine. "You're really something, you know that?"

I shrugged, not sure that I believed him. Sure it was a weird decision that could be seen as a good deed, but if he saw the file the social worker had on me he would probably change his mind.

We walked in silence back to the front of the Christmas Tree Farm, his shoulder brushing up against mine every now and again. Each time I could feel heat transfer from his body and into mine, despite the thick jacket he had on. It was surprisingly comforting. The boys I'd known in the past usually made me tremble in my boots, but Eli was so different.

His parents were waiting for us, a cup of warm apple cider in each of their hands. Eli presented the tree to Jan and Robert, standing it up in front of them. "This is our tree, Lottie picked it out."

Jan stared down at the tree, tilting her head back and forth. Maybe she was trying to see if it looked better from another angle, or picture how her decorations would look on such a shaggy tree. No matter, a bright smile appeared on her face. "I think it's perfect." She pulled me into a tight hug.

"You do?" Robert muttered under his breath as Jan's hand caught him right in the car. He cleared his throat, quickly correcting himself. "Right, we do."

"Thank you so much, Lottie, for coming with us and being apart of this tradition." She squeezed my hand.

My eyes locked with Eli's. I never noticed how deep his eyes were until that moment as they reflected against the sunlight. They were so easy to get lost in, like a deep-sea of beautiful emotions and memories all coming to the surface. My gaze flickered down to his lips briefly as his hand raised up to my cheek, moving a loose strand of hair away from my line of sight. My breath hitched in my throat. I felt as if a force was drawing us together, begging for his touch.

"Come on your two, let's pay and get this show on the road!" His mom's voice broke my trance and I quickly jumped back.

Eli brushed the back of his neck with his hand and my cheeks burned a light shade of pink. "Let's go."

CHAPTER 7

Cole Blackwood

The whole ride to my parents' house, I kept sneaking glances across the car, trying to gauge her reaction to what I thought was an almost kiss. I felt like we had a moment back there, and everything in me wanted it to be true. It seemed like a good sign that she hadn't shied away when I touched her hair, though I had expected her to. When I met her, she had practically jumped backward at the mere thought of me. Now, she was letting me touch her face. Oh, how I wanted to do more than touch her face.

Everything in me yearned to reach across and ask for her hand, but she seemed so unbothered by everything, I couldn't help but wonder if she really felt what I did. The mere thought of her rejecting me stopped me from reaching over and asking for what I most wanted. I hoped I wasn't giving her the wrong impression. I'd probably have a better chance of figuring that out if I could settle on what the wrong impression was.

By the time we reached my parents' house, I had completely convinced myself that Lottie had no interest in me beyond friendship, a place to stay, and a fix for her car. I mean, I had tried to convince myself of that. But looking over at her singing and dancing to the terrible radio station sportscasting had me seriously questioning that decision.

"So, shall we go in, Maestro?" I shouted to be heard, "or do you need to sing more sports scores?"

She stopped suddenly and sank back into her seat and I immediately knew I had done something wrong. With my words, I had pressed one of those open wounds she carried. Though she hid them well, I knew they were there.

"I'm sorry," I looked down to avoid looking at her face. "I didn't mean anything by it. . . I was just trying to poke fun."

"Of course you were, Maestro." She smiled at me as I looked up at her. "I was just poking fun, too."

I could have let myself believe that were true, but the sadness beneath the surface pierced through her eyes. She seemed like she wanted me to drop it, so I decided against apologizing.

"Oh, you're good at that!" I tried to dig myself out of the hole. "Are you ready for my mother's famous Sunday dinner?"

"Only if there are marshmallows for the hot chocolate." She playfully tapped my arm before we got out of the truck. "I was promised marshmallows for my hot chocolate."

"I don't think my mother has ever met a marshmallow challenge she didn't win," I caught up with Lottie just as we reached the door, "But I'd like to see you try."

Oh no, I had let the flirt out again. Put that away, Blackwood.

I was spared whatever awkwardness might have come out of my mouth next by my mom opening the door and pulling Lottie into a huge hug.

"Lottie! I'm so glad you could join us for dinner. I do miss having a house full."

She barely acknowledged me as she swept Lottie into the house, giving her the grand tour of the space I had grown up in. I was internally grateful that I had cleaned out my room earlier this year, sparing me from watching her investigate my childhood room.

I closed the door and took off my coat and shoes before searching the house for Lottie and my mom.

I finally found them on the advice of my dad - they were in the kitchen. I peeked in and watched their interactions without making my presence known.

The first thing I saw was Lottie stirring the gravy under my mom's watchful eye.

"Am I doing this right?" Lottie looked up at my mom with a look I couldn't describe.

"It's perfect, dear," my mom smiled kindly at Lottie, "you have a real knack for this. Do you have any cooking specialties?"

Lottie laughed as she stirred the gravy, "I usually don't burn my mac and cheese! But I'm worried I might burn this gravy."

"Nonsense, dear," my mom put her arm around Lottie's shoulder, "You are doing great."

"It's fun to learn, but I think I'd be more comfortable if you took over. Is there any fruit I can cut or something?" Lottie handed the spoon back, "I'm very good at cutting fruit."

Mom laughed as she took the spoon from Lottie and laid it beside the stove, "I think we can find something you're more comfortable doing."

I tried to go back to the living room and watch whatever real crime show my dad was watching, but my mom must have noticed I was there.

"Cole!" she called out, "Can you come in here and help Lottie, please?"

She really knew how to make me help her. How could I say no to helping Lottie?

I waited a minute before stepping into the kitchen, "Yes, Mom. What do you need help with?"

The look on her face said *I know you've been watching us this whole time* but she only said, "I think Lottie was looking to cut some fruit for dinner."

I grabbed some fruit, a cutting board, and two knives and helped Lottie cut some oranges and strawberries. I'm not sure that's what my mom had in mind when she asked for fruit, but it's what I like. When we finished, Lottie decided we needed some blueberries, so she washed some and added them to our selection while I cleaned up the mess we had made.

I hadn't even finished putting the cutting board into the sink when mom decided it was dinner time. "Robert, it's time for dinner!" she called out the door of the kitchen. When he didn't respond and I heard mom's footsteps down the hallway, I started giggling.

"What's so funny?" Lottie looked at me with her brows furrowed. It was only then I realized I had been staring at her even as I listened to my mom.

"Oh, it's not you, it's -" I didn't have to finish my explanation. I just gestured with my hand towards the sound of my mother's voice coming down the hallway.

"Robert! I shouldn't have to yell so loud the next town can hear me just to get you to come to supper," she walked in pulling my dad by his hand, as though he were a small child.

"I could hear you, I just don't move that fast anymore."

She let go of his arm and rolled her eyes, "Don't move that fast because you wanted to see the end of the play is more like it."

She turned and addressed Lottie, who was struggling to keep her laugh inside, resulting in a rather weird grimace on her face.

"Are you alright, dear?" Mom looked at Lottie with the same look she gave me every time I was home sick from school, "I can get you some water."

Lottie pulled herself together. "Water would be lovely. But really, I'm fine." She returned my mom's kind smile and sat down to eat.

❆❆❆

"I think that's the first time in a long time that I haven't had to talk about myself at family dinner." I smiled at Lottie as we went on a tour of the front room. Mom had insisted I show her since she had apparently missed it in her tour of the house earlier.

My mother never misses anything.

"I like your family," she smiled back and walked towards the mantle over the fireplace.

"I like them too," I followed her, trying to figure out what had caught her eye, "most days, at least."

"It must have been nice growing up here," she ran her hand along the ornate frame holding our most recent family photograph. "Was it?"

She looked back at me with a gaze so intense, I didn't know what to do.

"Uhh . . ." I stuttered a bit, "I mean, yeah it was pretty nice. It's like any family, you know? Sometimes they drive you nuts, but I guess they love you so you let them do it. Parents are always doing stuff to get on your nerves. But it's better now that I'm older and moved out. I can make the small decisions for myself, but still, come over and eat a home-cooked meal and get yelled at by my mom every once in a while."

Lottie was eerily silent, and I wondered if I should say something. I decided to just join her in staring at the family Christmas photo in the gold frame on the left side of our mantle. Mom already had some of the decorations out, so it was flanked by a snowman plushie and a reindeer snow globe.

We were silent for way too long as she stared at the photo on the mantle. Some stupid part of me who knows no boundaries reached out and took her hand as we stood there. To my surprise, she accepted it.

We stood there hand in hand as she quietly whispered, "I don't."

"You don't, what?" I was always asking questions in the worst way.

"I don't know what it's like to have a family."

I stood there, holding Lottie's hand, completely frozen. There were a million things running through my head. I desperately wanted to know what she meant, but I didn't want to ask any more questions that would hurt her.

"It's okay," she said before I could say anything, "you don't have to say anything."

"I'm sorry," I blurted out.

We both looked at each other.

"I mean, I don't know what to say, but I'm sorry." I felt the heat rise in my cheeks and subconsciously touched my neck in embarrassment.

Lottie cleared her throat. "So, what's going on in this picture, exactly?"

I looked where she was pointing. "We were making Christmas cookies."

"Is that how you got covered in drywall dust?" she raised her eyebrow at me.

"It's flour, Lottie!" I resisted the urge to pull her in closer and kiss her forehead. "Not all of us are fabulous chefs!"

"Oh, I'd love to see that!" she laughed and pulled my arm around her back so I was holding her.

"I'd love to show you," I pulled her slightly closer and rested my head on hers as we looked at the collection of family photos.

"It's a date."

Had I heard her correctly? I turned her towards me slightly and, for the second time in three hours, my mother set me up with the girl I liked only to interrupt us when we were finally about to kiss.

"Treats for the road!" she sang as she rounded the corner with a plastic container filled with cake. "Please remember to bring me the container back, will you?"

Lottie and I hugged Mom and promised to bring the container back before making our way home for the night.

This time, after I got into the car, I reached over for Lottie's hand.

And this time, while we drove, we both danced and sang along to the music. I felt happier than I had in a long time. She brought out something in me that was pure joy.

I walked her to her room still holding her hand. When we got to the door, I gave her a kiss on the cheek.

"I had a really fun time today." I wanted to kiss her again. "I'm glad we went."

"Me too." She tucked a strand of hair behind her ear. "Thanks for letting me tag along."

She opened the door and started walking inside, still holding my hand. I pulled her back towards me for a hug.

"Goodnight," I whispered into her ear before letting go of her hand and walking back towards the couch. By the look on Lottie's face, I think that might have been a very big mistake.

CHAPTER 8

Charlotte Sweet

I must have tossed and turned for hours the night before, thinking about the moment I shared with Eli. His touch sent my body into a frenzy. It had been so long since I had felt someone's warmth and it was lonely, but it was the life I led. The second he let go, I felt his absence.

In two days, I felt more connected to Eli than people I'd known for years at school or the foster families I'd spent time with. I crossed a line that I promised myself years ago I wouldn't, I got attached. The foster system taught me how to lock my feelings away and compartmentalize because I knew it was only a matter of time before the other shoe would drop and I'd have to leave.

I never expected that I'd like it here, maybe that was how I let my emotions creep in.

Lying in bed, I could still feel his touch lingering on my fingertips and the small of my back. Tears slipped down my cheeks as shame ruminated in the pit of my stomach. I came here for a reason and needed to focus on fixing my car so I could get back on the road.

There was a knock on the door and I quickly wiped the tears away before Eli stuck his head in. "Can I come in to get my clothes for work?"

"Yeah, of course, it's your room." I rolled out of bed and wrapped a blanket around myself. He rummaged through his dresser, opening numerous drawers until he found what he was looking for. "When do you think the part will come in for my car?"

"Hopefully by Wednesday but with the weather around here it's hard to be sure, especially with Christmas right around the corner." He turned back to me and gave me a sympathetic smile. "I'll get it done as soon as the part comes in. I know you're anxious to get back on the road."

Was it that obvious? I could almost feel the tension between us as we stared into each other's eyes. Somehow he seemed to know exactly what was wrong without asking.

"I'll give you a ride to the cafe on my way to work." He walked back to the door, lingering momentarily before shutting it behind him.

I sat back down on the bed and sighed, knowing that even if there was a possibility of our friendship blossoming into something more he would never like a girl with a past like mine. "Time to get ready," I told myself.

My bag of clothes was starting to look smaller and smaller the longer I stayed. Anything with holes or that was see-through I definitely couldn't wear around Eli's mother. After eliminating those from my already small wardrobe, I was left with one black dress that I wore to a foster father's funeral two years ago. It was a hand-me-down and hardly work appropriate.

As I slipped it on, it hung on my body, no better than a paper bag and was two sizes too big. I grunted, slamming my foot against the hardwood flooring.

The bedroom door burst open as Eli ran in, concerned. He relaxed once he saw I was okay, but his eyes trailed my body with a displeased look. "What are you wearing?" he asked, holding in a chuckle.

I frowned. "Don't tease, I have nothing else to wear."

He thought for a second before scurrying out of the room, returning with a blue bag full of clothes. "My sister asked me to drop these off in the donation bin but I haven't gotten around to it. You can see if anything fits. I'll just be in the kitchen if you need anything."

I opened the bag once Eli left and rifled through. His sister had good taste in clothes. I could tell she wasn't giving them away because they were worn, she just probably didn't wear them anymore. A sweater with a white collared shirt sewn in caught my attention. It was just what I pictured someone working in a cozy cafe would wear.

I threw my dress to the side and quickly got changed into a pair of jeans, slipping the sweater over my head. I glanced at myself in the mirror and saw the girl I wanted to be staring back at me. A small smile pulled at my lips before I headed into the kitchen to meet Eli.

He turned to face me, sticking a spoonful of cereal into his mouth. "You look great," he mumbled, his mouth full.

"Thanks," I said, leaning back against the wall. My stomach grumbled loudly in my ears and I hoped to god it wasn't loud enough for Eli to hear. A light shade of pink coated my cheeks.

"Would you like something for breakfast before we go?" He spun around and pulled out two boxes of cereal and a bag of bagels. "These are the options. If you don't like those, I can pick something up at the store on my way home from work."

"No no, these are great. I'll just have some Honey Nut Cheerios," I told him, a smile tugging at my lips. I wasn't used to someone going out of their way to make me feel welcome and cared for. It was nice but at the same time, I felt a pang of guilt in the pit of my stomach for making him go to such lengths to accommodate me. I didn't want to be a bother.

We ate in silence, every once in a while gazing over at one another. I knew I would have to repay him and his family somehow for their hospitality, but I didn't have anything to give. I didn't have any money or valuable objects, just my thanks and I wasn't sure if that would be enough.

It made me want to collect my things and run away, but I had no car to make my escape in and nowhere to run away to. I didn't like owing people favors, I wasn't a charity case. Time after time Eli made me forget that I didn't actually belong here but the reality kept seeping back in.

I stared down at the bowl and sighed. Eli kept glancing over at the clock on the microwave and his knee bounced up and down. The voice in my head kept telling me that I was going to make him late for work. I gulped down the last few bites and stood up abruptly.

"Should we go?" I asked, collecting my things.

Eli's bowl made a clunking sound as he placed it in the sink before rinsing my now empty bowl. He nodded and followed me toward the door. "Let's go."

Stepping out into the cold, I immediately wanted to run back inside and huddle under the covers. Eli's hand lingered on the small of my back. I glanced up at his face, seeing the small smile he wore as we trod through the snow. It seemed like a subconscious action, something normal he would do with all of his friends. Whereas I found myself trying to read his thoughts and find an ulterior motive, but I found none.

He was just a good guy and it seemed impossible not to put my trust in him.

❄❄❄

Light acoustic music played in the background as I wiped down the tables at the end of the night. The last few stragglers were making their way out the door making small talk with Jan.

Eli hadn't left my mind all day. The way he spoke and moved, the way he was so willing to help. It baffled me and I spent all day trying to figure out what made him such a good human being.

"Alright dear, I'm calling it a night." She sighed and flipped over the open sign before taking a seat in front of me. I let myself relax knowing that the job was done at least until tomorrow. "Are you waiting for Cole to pick you up?"

"Yeah, he's probably just closing up." I tucked my pad of paper in my apron as Jan patted the table, gesturing for me to sit down.

"Let's have a little chat," she suggested. Hesitantly I sat down, fearing the next words that would come out of her mouth. "It's alright, I just want to know more about the sweet girl who's spending time with my son."

Maybe there's nothing to know, I thought.

"Why do you say that?" She leaned in closer, taking my hand. I quickly realized I'd said it out loud and not just in my head. My breath hitched as I began to panic.

"No reason, I'm sorry." I bit down on my lip, making sure any more of my thoughts didn't slip out of my mouth.

She patted my hand and smiled sympathetically. "Tell me about yourself."

I gulped down the lump in my throat as I began to work out what I was going to say. There were so many versions of the story that I'd made up about growing up with a happy family with doctors or captains of industries for parents. The girls at school always got a kick out of it, although something in me said that I couldn't lie to Eli's mother.

"I was born in Charlotte, North Carolina, but I moved around a lot as a kid. I graduated high school last year. I decided to go on a road trip and my car broke down. That's when Eli found me." It was vague, but at least it was the truth.

"Charlotte, born in Charlotte," she said with a smile and began to nod silently as if taking in the information. Whoever named me, wasn't very clever. Or maybe they thought they were, which would have been even worse. "Were your parents in the military?"

"No," I muttered and stood up, the chair screeching against the tile floor. "Maybe we should call Eli, see if he's on his way?"

The cafe door opened, making the bell ring and Eli stepped in. "Sorry I'm late, lost track of time."

"No problem." I collected my things and rushed to his side. "We better get going, right?"

I looked up at him, wondering if he could see the desperation and panic. Whether or not he could, he agreed. "Yeah, got big plans for supper tonight." Eli stepped forward and gave his mom a kiss on the cheek. "See you tomorrow."

Her eyes stayed locked with mine as she offered a sweet smile. "Have a good night."

I followed Eli out into the cold, zipping up my jacket. I could tell something was on his mind by the way he walked slightly ahead of me, his eyes looking up at the stars. Although he waited until we got into the truck before he said anything.

"Did something happen with my mom? Did she say something to you?"

A frown slipped onto my face. Causing a rift between Eli and his mom was the last thing I wanted. Their relationship was everything I wanted with a mother. "No, I'm just tired that's all. It's been a long day."

"Okay," he muttered, moving his hand so it was lying on top of mine. "Let's go home."

I felt butterflies dance in my stomach at the thought. *Home. If only.*

CHAPTER 9

Cole Blackwood

After I dropped Lottie off at the diner for work, I raced to the shop so I could beat Joe and get a jump on my work for the day. I was trying to get enough done that I could take a break for supper and go to the diner. Lottie lingered in my mind the whole day as I ran through diagnostics, changed the oil, filed paperwork, and other equally exciting parts of my job. By 11 am, Joe was already getting on me to speed up.

"Eli," he shouted from across the shop. "What am I paying you for?"

"Making cotton candy and popcorn at the annual town parade," I shouted back, my head under the hood of the car I was working on.

"No!" He laughed at my joke. "Okay, well, yes. But also to fix the cars, not to dream about pretty young ladies we find on the side of the road."

I backed up out of the car so fast that I stumbled backward over a hose and tripped into a garbage can filled with very dirty rags. Before I could reply to Joe's assumption, I was flat on my back on the floor of the shop, covered head to toe in trash.

"Great." I sat up and brushed myself off. "I'm a mess."

"Hazard of the job, Eli." Joe threw me a towel from a few feet away. "Go wash up and take your lunch. See you back here in half an hour."

I mumbled various profanities under my breath as I walked towards the bathroom to wash off my face and hands.

"Leave your suit in the wash pile, Eli," Joe shouted before I opened the door to the bathroom. "Don't spread that mess around any more than you already have."

I shrugged out of it, revealing my tee-shirt and jeans, before washing and heading out to lunch.

"Coat!" Joe called after me as I pushed open the front door. "Honestly, Eli, you'd forget your head if it weren't attached. Figure out whatever's going on there or you'll be run over by your own truck."

"Yeah, thanks." I threw on my coat and ran out the door and across the lot to my truck. No way was I going to see Lottie looking like this, so I ate the sandwich I had packed while I sat in the backseat of the truck.

When I did go back into the shop, Joe pretended he hadn't seen me eating in my truck and sent me back to work for the remainder of the afternoon.

It was all going fine until we were about to close up. As I walked past Lottie's car with the last of my paperwork, I had a sudden urge to look inside. I desperately wanted to learn everything about her, and looking in her car seemed like a great way to do it.

I hesitated before deciding to close the door. As I leaned in to shut the door, I noticed something had rolled off the backseat and onto the floor. Putting my knee on her front seat, I was able to reach through and pick up a small, brown teddy bear that looked like it was at least as old as Lottie. Maybe older.

This didn't seem like something I should be leaving in the shop overnight, so I tucked it into my coat to take home with me. Maybe I could give it to Lottie once I figured out how to tell her I was digging around in her car.

"Lock up when you leave," Joe said as he walked past. "And don't stay too late. I was only joking about you not working hard enough."

I'm not sure he was joking, exactly, but it was nice that he cared about me. "Yeah, I'm just hanging around until Lottie's done her shift. I'm going to drive her home."

"Of course you are," he said as he waved and left through the closing garage door. I made my way to the office and sat down with a book to fill the time.

It wasn't until my phone alarm went off that I realized how late it was. I must have fallen asleep in the chair, though my book was somehow still in my hands.

Racing out to my truck, I completely forgot the bear was even in my pocket until I went to put my seatbelt on. Not seeing anywhere else to stash it without Lottie seeing it, I decided to leave it in my pocket as I turned on the truck and drove as fast as I could to pick Lottie up from the diner.

I parked halfway on the sidewalk and ran in through the door of the cafe. "Sorry I'm late, lost track of time."

"No problem." Lottie smiled and practically ran over to me. "We better get going, right?"

What is up with her? I couldn't tell what was going on, so I decided to agree with her. "Yeah, got big plans for supper tonight."

I could hear Mom and Lottie saying things to me as I tried to keep up my half of the conversation, but I couldn't think of anything besides how I was going to tell Lottie about the tiny little bear pressed into my chest.

❄❄❄

We didn't really have any big dinner plans, so after I took a quick shower, I made some soup and grilled cheese while Lottie got changed out of her work clothes and took a shower of her own. *Try not to focus on that, Eli.*

When she came out of the room wearing a cute little dress, I'm pretty sure a 'wow' slipped out of my mouth as she made her way to the kitchen. As we ate, my eyes constantly wandered between Lottie and my jacket draped over the back of the couch like an ominous monster. *If she finds it before I tell her . . .*

"Lottie?" I decided to broach the subject as we were finishing up our dinner and grabbing chips for our movie marathon.

"Yeah?" she asked as she reached up into the cabinet to find a bowl for the chips. I watched the hem of her skirt lift a little as she stood on her toes to reach.

"Uh... Oh! I found something today in your car." *That's not how I meant to start this conversation.*

She froze, arm still raised above her head holding the largest bowl I owned. "What did you find?"

"I didn't mean to snoop, I was just walking by and I saw him lying there and . . ." I'm sure I kept babbling on as I picked up my jacket and took out the small, matted stuffed animal. I turned to face her. "I found this and I thought it might be important to you because it didn't look like something you should have left behind and-"

The next thing I knew, the bowl fell to the ground as Lottie ran across my apartment and into my arms.

"Oh, I can't believe you found him! I thought I'd lost him forever!" She was somehow hugging the bear and me at the same time.

I probably should have said something, but I was too busy enjoying the smell of her hair and the closeness of her hug to really *do* anything.

When she let me go, I desperately wanted to pull her back into the hug, but I felt like I'd scare her off. *I always feel like I'll scare her off. Like one false move will send her packing and I'll never see her again. And the more I get to know her, the more it hurts to think of her leaving.*

"So, who is this fine young fellow?" I asked, trying to behave normally. "Does he have a name?"

"Herbert." She was sitting on the couch staring at him as she spoke to me. "My birth mom gave him to me."

I sat down on the other side of the couch, trying to play it cool. I had no idea what to say. *Birth Mom?*

I was only capable of looking at her as she slowly raised her eyes up to meet mine over the top of Herbert's head. In them, I saw something I'm not used to with her. She looked scared. Vulnerable.

I was drawn into her as I slowly moved closer to her and rested my hand on hers. I let my eyes gaze into hers for a few moments before I found the words to reply. "She must have really loved you."

There were tears in Lottie's eyes, threatening to spill over as she softly answered me. "She did, I think. In her own way, I think she did."

I reached over to offer her a hug and, to my surprise, she accepted. I pulled her in beside me and wrapped my arms around her as she cried into my shirt. I smoothed her hair on top of her head and placed a kiss on her forehead as I hugged her and she hugged Herbert.

Neither one of us said anything as I held her, though she quickly stopped crying and started smiling. I looked down at her when she let out a small laugh.

"I've never actually told anyone that before." She looked up to me, her face dangerously close to mine. "I can't believe I told you that!"

"Herbert's secret is safe with me." I was trying to think of something else to say when I noticed her slowly lifting her head towards mine.

My mind was screaming that I should not get involved with this girl who was leaving in two days, but I ignored it and closed the gap between us with a tentative kiss.

Lottie quickly took matters into her own hands as Herbert fell to the floor and both of Lottie's hands found the back of my head, pulling me towards her and deepening our kiss. All I could think about at that moment was how long I'd been wishing for her to kiss me, and how out of practice I was. Everything else melted away as I leaned into her soft lips.

When she let me go, I desperately wanted to kiss her again, but she had turned her head away as she reached down to pick up Herbert.

Not knowing what to do with the silence between us, I decided to ask the question burning on my mind. "Lottie? You mentioned your birth mom. What happened to her?"

"I don't know exactly." Lottie stared sadly at her hands. "I just know I was shuffled to a foster home and then some other stuff happened and here I am."

"So you didn't like your adoptive parents?" I asked her, hoping to learn more about her family.

Her face twisted up in pain. "I uh, never had adoptive parents, actually. If you don't mind I think I'm just going to go to bed."

I didn't want to let her go, but I knew I didn't have a choice. How had I let the night go from amazing to terrible with only two questions?

"Yeah. Okay, goodnight Lottie." I tried to smile but I was almost in tears. She was already down the hallway when I whispered, "I'm sorry" but I was almost certain she couldn't hear me.

I was debating whether it was worth it to ask her to let me in to get clothes when I heard the door to my room open again. I stood up from the couch and walked into the hallway where I could see her. She stepped into the hallway, already dressed in her pajamas, and sheepishly looked at me.

"Eli?" her voice was tender and soft. "I'm sorry. I'm not used to talking to people about this. I want to tell you, I'm just not sure I'm ready yet."

"I understand." I closed the space between us to give her a hug, "I'll be here when you are ready."

As she ended our hug, she slid her hand down my arm until she was holding my hand.

"Will you stay with me? Just for a little while?"

This time, I wasn't stupid enough to say no as she gently pulled my hand towards her. I only meant to stay until she fell asleep, but as I lay there holding her sleep pulled me under.

CHAPTER 10

Charlotte Sweet

As I woke up, I slowly began to feel a weight around my waist and a warmth radiating through me. My eyes fluttered open to see Eli still lying next to me, fast asleep. I snuggled further into his chest and pulled the covers up around me as the cold morning air nipped at my skin. My lips tingled as I remembered the kiss we shared, how it made butterflies dance in the pit of my stomach and all my thoughts disappear. But they weren't absent now.

Part of me expected Eli to run for the hills when I told him about never being adopted. He had to be thinking, *what's so wrong with her that no one ever wanted her?* It's what I thought for the majority of my life.

My stuffed bear, Herbert brought back so many memories. He was there for it, every sleepless night and every tear. He reminded me that there was someone out there who loved me and Eli brought him back to me.

I closed my eyes and sighed, waiting for the other shoe to drop and for my world to be torn out from under me. As much as I liked it here, I knew that it couldn't last forever. Eli would decide that I wasn't enough for him, that where I came from made me too different. Even if he didn't I'd still be leaving when my car was fixed and I wasn't sure I'd come back.

One of us was bound to get hurt. It was inevitable.

Eli began to stir and his arm tightened around my waist. Suddenly I felt trapped and the familiar urge to run away.

"Morning beautiful," he whispered as his eyes flickered open. My body relaxed as I heard his voice and looked into his eyes. *Maybe this time is different,* I told myself. Of course, I'd caught myself thinking those exact words a thousand times before. "What time is it?"

I looked across him and over at the clock that was sitting on the nightstand. "It's quarter after seven."

He groaned and kissed the top of my head before pulling himself out of bed. "We should get ready for work."

I watched as he walked to the closet and picked out clothes for the day. For a second Eli glanced back at me, his eyes locking with mine. Blush cascaded onto my cheeks and I pulled the blankets up over my smiling face, embarrassed. In the past, I'd never let a guy have such an effect on me but a few days with Eli and my walls were crashing down.

He noticed and climbed back into bed, pulling the sheets away from my face. "I love when you smile," he muttered, giving me a wink. His comment only made me blush more.

"Eli," my voice was barely audible as I spoke and my heart began to race. I reached forward and laid my hand on his chest, pushing him back slightly.

"Too much too fast?" he sounded understanding but I couldn't help but notice the disappointment on his face as I nodded. Although, it was quick to disappear as he sat back. "It's okay, I get it. It hasn't been that long and we still don't know a lot about each other, so let's get to know each other."

"I like the sound of that." I leaned forward and placed a kiss on his cheek. "Now we have to get ready for work or we'll be late."

I feared he wasn't going to be the first one to turn away, so I hopped off the bed and scooped up my clothes only glancing back momentarily before going into the washroom.

As I looked in the mirror, I realized I didn't recognize the girl that was staring back at me. My skin was full of warmth and my cheeks had a slight pink tinge. The smile I wore on my face felt genuine and almost hurt, it was so big. I liked this me and I wished it could be this way forever. For someone who had moved around and had zero stability all her life, I couldn't help but wonder how I let myself get so attached. Maybe it was the people, maybe it was the Christmas spirit in the air. I wasn't sure of the answer.

I quickly got dressed and threw my hair up in a messy bun. Semi presentable was always my go-to but it didn't seem good enough now. I wanted to look my best, like other girls my age who had money to spend on fancy hair and makeup products, but it would have to do.

I took one last glance in the mirror before I left the bathroom and met Eli in the kitchen, nerves filling my belly. He even looked good in his dirty, greased up mechanic clothes. A thick sheet of blush covered my cheeks, but Eli didn't seem to notice. He held out a box of cereal and a bowl. "Do you want some breakfast?"

I shook my head, "I'm not hungry. I think I'll just wait until lunch." Maybe by then I'd have his image out of my head and feel like myself again.

"Okay if you say so," he muttered. "Everything alright?"

"Yeah, of course," I lied. But I didn't know a time when I'd actually answered that question truthfully. Eli smiled and stepped toward me, resting his hand on my waist. Apparently I was more convincing than I thought because he didn't say another word.

His hand trailed down my arm and he intertwined our fingers. Eli leaned over and pulled my jacket off the hook. "Let's go," he instructed and put my jacket on for me.

He was quiet on the ride to work and turned on the music, humming along to the melody. The entire time his hand stayed locked on mine as if he thought at any second I'd bolt. The truck came to a rolling stop outside of his mom's cafe. He shifted into park and turned to face me.

"I'll pick you up here afterward," he said but didn't let me go.

"You have to let go of my hand first."

His eyes flickered down to our hands and nodded, letting go. "Oh right. Well, I'll see you later."

Eli looked so cute while he was pouting at me. Slowly I leaned in, about to kiss him. He knew what I had in mind and closed the distance. His lips touched mine gently as his hands cupped my cheeks, setting a fire in the pit of my stomach. Our lips parted and I rested my forehead against his.

"I'll see you later." I smiled and opened the passenger door, hopping out of the truck. "Thanks Eli."

The cold air nipped at my skin as I crossed the street but the second I stepped into the cafe I was overcome by warmth. Jan rounded the corner from the kitchen and smiled. "Good morning darling, we have a busy day ahead of us."

"Good morning," I mumbled and ducked into the backroom to get an apron. I felt awkward knowing that I just made out with her son not five minutes ago. Tying it around my waist, I walked back into the main area as Jan flipped the sign to open.

The day dragged on slowly as people came and went, each one having their own conversation with Jan. From the inside of the cafe, I was starting to see how small a town this really was. Everyone seemed to have their own theory about me and why I was here but Jan shut each and every one of them down. Probably because most had to do with Eli after we held hands at the Christmas tree farm. I tried not to listen but it was hard not to.

If something happened between Eli and me each and every one of these people would know, especially if I broke his heart.

A toddler crying broke me out of my thoughts and made me spin around. With living in so many foster homes, I'd seen it all. I'd been the maid and the babysitter while the parents were the ones getting paid by the state. While I wished that their parents were more invested in their lives, I liked kids and I was good with them.

A young mother with two young kids was packing up her things, getting them dressed to brave the cold while one screamed and thrashed. She looked frustrated and exhausted, yet no one jumped up to give her a hand. Everyone was too wrapped up in their own lives.

"Let me give you a hand," I told her, bending down to pick up the soother that was on the ground and tucked it into the diaper bag.

She smiled, graciously as she bounced the little girl on her shoulder. "Thank you, that would be great actually."

I made a silly face, taking the little girl's attention off of the jacket that was being put over her arms. She had to be just over one year old. The crying stopped and she watched me intently as I started a game of peek-a-boo. A smile tugged at my lips as she started to giggle.

"Would you mind holding her for a second?" the mother asked.

I shook my head. "No, not at all."

She placed her in my arms and I immediately mimicked the bouncing motion her mom had been using. Her little hands reached forward and wrapped around the chain of my necklace, mesmerized with the tiny teacup hanging from it. I fell in love with it at a tiny consignment antique store and bartered it down to a measly ten dollars.

The mom dressed the little boy, who looked to be about three years old and helped him down from the chair. She picked up the diaper bag and slung it over her shoulder before turning back to me with open arms. I handed her, her daughter.

"Thank you for your help," she said and headed toward the door. My eyes followed and landed on Eli.

He strode toward me, smiling brightly. "Hey," he muttered as his hand brushed against the small of my back. "You're really good with kids."

I tucked a strand of hair behind my ear. "I've had a lot of practice." The minute it came out of my mouth I knew it'd give him the wrong impression.

He furrowed his brows, confused by my statement but he didn't say anything more as his mom walked up to us. She gently kissed his cheek. "You're here early."

"I finished up at work and thought I'd stop by and see if I could steal Lottie for the rest of the day." He nudged my shoulder.

"Oh? Something special planned?" Jan pried for more information from her son.

"Actually I wanted to teach her your Christmas cookie recipe if that's okay," he mentioned and I tilted my head up to look at him, wondering why I hadn't been informed about these special plans.

"Of course you can, I can definitely handle things here for the rest of the day. Go! Have fun!" She pretty much pushed us toward the door and handed me my jacket.

"Bye mom," Eli chuckled and helped me find the arm of my jacket.

"Thanks, Jan." I waved goodbye as falling snow hit me in the face. I pointed in Eli's direction. "Don't you dare laugh."

He held his hands up in surrender. "I'm not laughing." It was true but I caught a glimpse at the goofy grin on his face. Suddenly, he wrapped his arms around my waist and pulled me toward the truck. "I kept it running for you." Like a gentleman, he opened the passenger door for me before jogging around to the driver's side.

"Thank you," I smiled while rubbing my hands together. "So what's the plan?"

"I told you, we are going to make cookies. It's a part of the Blackwood family Christmas tradition." He winked and then pulled out onto the road.

"Well, I'd be honored to help."

"Good," he said and glanced my direction briefly before bringing his eyes back to the street. The crossing light flickered on and the truck came to a stop. A kid skipped across the road, waving an orange caution sign as his parents followed close behind. "What did you mean earlier when you said you'd had a lot of practice with kids?" He tapped his hands against the steering wheel and sighed. "Do you have a kid?"

"Oh... no, sometimes the homes I was in had young kids and I'd help take care of them. It's not a big deal really, I like kids. Sorry I gave you the wrong impression." I laughed, trying to fill the awkward silence that followed.

"It'd be okay if you did, I'd understand..." He forced a smile and as the family reached the sidewalk he started back down the road. "Well let's go home and make some cookies."

CHAPTER 11

Cole Blackwood

The whole drive home, I couldn't stop turning to look at Lottie. Every time we passed under a streetlight, her hair shone a little more red than I'd ever seen it before. She'd ignored my making a complete idiot of myself and was laughing and dancing to the music.

When I stretched my hand over to hold hers, she teased me a little but obliged. She was radiant and I was trying not to be terrified that she would leave. A small part of me knew she would. As soon as I finish her car, all of this could end. Somehow that knowledge both excited and terrified me.

"So, what kind of cookies are we making?" Lottie asked once the truck was parked.

I hopped out of the truck and jogged around to open her door for her. She smiled just as she had when we left the cafe and my heart fluttered in my chest. I took her hand and helped her out of the truck. "We're making Christmas cookies, of course."

I closed the door of the truck and walked towards the door.

"Yes," she said, sliding her arm around my shoulder. "But how does one make Christmas cookies?"

I turned to look at her and found her forehead brushing my lips, so I kissed her forehead and wrapped my own arm around her back, pulling her closer. "That's what I'm going to teach you today."

When we got to the door, I stopped and directed Lottie to stand facing the door with her eyes closed. I'd skipped out on work today to get ready for this cookie tradition, and I was trying to make it as fun for Lottie as I could.

"What are you doing?" she asked me, her eyes questioning and worried.

"Just trust me," I squeezed her hand and kissed her cheek. "It's a good surprise."

She blushed at my touch and closed her eyes, covering them with her free hand.

"Now, we'll have to go very slowly, because I don't want you to fall down any stairs."

She nodded and I led her inside by the hand, carefully stepping backward down the stairs until she had reached the bottom. I urged her a little further until she was standing in front of the counter. Making sure her eyes were still closed, I pulled away the tea towel to reveal the gift I had gotten her.

I took a deep breath and held her hand a little tighter, "Okay, you can open your eyes."

She peeked through her fingers first, before taking her hand away completely to inspect the Christmas apron and reindeer antler headband laid out on the counter.

"Wow," she smiled at me and all my nerves left my body. I wrapped my arm around her waist as she drew her finger along the embroidery on the apron, and a few tears seemed to be pooling in the corner of her eyes.

"I hope you like it," I said, feeling the shaky feeling return to my arms. "I had them put Lottie on it. The reindeer antlers are just because this girl at the store said they're fun apparently." I could feel myself about to blabber away the awkward silence, so I pushed my lips together to stop oversharing.

She picked the apron up off the counter and placed it over her head, turning around so I could reach the ties. As she handed me the ties she said, "No. I love it. I don't know if I've ever owned anything with my name on it before."

I should have thought of that. Why do I always make things harder for Lottie, no matter what I do? I tried not to let my face drop. "Well, let's not forget the reindeer headband to complete your look." She pulled her hair back into a ponytail and then let me place the antlers on her head.

"So is this how you make cookies, then?" she asked me. "Or was that whole cookie thing just an excuse to give me this very early Christmas present?"

"Oh no! We are definitely making cookies." I turned around to open the drawer that contained my own, well-loved Christmas apron and a cheap Santa hat. Once I'd put them on, I turned to face her. "What do you think?"

She chuckled and reached up to move the pom-pom of the hat out of my face, "I think you look ridiculous!" She moved to walk around me and her eyes fell on the front of my apron. Her eyes softened and she lifted her arm to trace the letters of my own apron.

"Cole," she said, tracing the letters again. "But you don't like Cole, you like Eli."

I nodded and brought my hand to the back of my neck, "Yeah, uh. It's actually. My mom got it for me when I first learned to make cookies with her." I didn't risk looking at her. "It's a Blackwood Family tradition."

She was silent for a moment while I watched my shoes. Eventually, I couldn't take it anymore and braved a quick glance at her face. She smiled softly and reached her arms around me for a hug. She lingered for a moment before pulling away and putting her hands on her hips.

"So, now that we are properly outfitted for the task, what's next?" She smiled as though nothing had happened. Part of me loved that about her because we never had awkward moments. But another part of me was beginning to see it for what it really was and the thought of Lottie putting on a happy face when she wasn't happy worried me more than anything else about her. How would I ever really know what she thought if she only ever smiles through everything? She's going to be a tough one.

I shook my head and focused on Lottie, "Well, next we make cookies!" I pulled out the binder my mom had given me with all of my favourite recipes and flipped to the page with her Christmas sugar cookies. "We have sugar cookies," I flipped the page, "or gingerbread."

"Which one's easier?"

"Probably sugar cookies," I shrugged. "But neither is very difficult."

"Sugar cookies it is!" she flipped the page back and began reading the instructions.

I managed to catch myself before I asked, 'you mean you've never made cookies before?'. Instead, choosing to pull the ingredients out of the cupboards so Lottie could start her baking.

She read through the ingredients and then the instructions twice, running her finger down the page as she went to make sure she didn't miss anything. "Okay, I'm ready," she declared, turning to face me. "I need a large bowl."

I acted as her sous chef, passing her the butter and sugar, before showing her how to use the mixer to cream her butter and sugar.

She was a natural, mixing everything together with ease and not struggling with eggshells in her mixture even once. By the time she stirred in the dry ingredients, both of our aprons were thoroughly covered in flour.

"Is it done?" she looked up at me. "Because to me it looks done."

I balled up the dough and placed it on the plastic wrap on the counter, "Yeah, it looks good."

"So, what's next?" she bounced across the kitchen to read Mom's recipe. I waited for her to find the next direction.

"Oh," she whined, "we're at the part where we have to chill it for like an hour!"

While the dough chilled, we cleaned up the kitchen, and ourselves, as much as possible. When we finished cleaning the whole kitchen, it still hadn't been an hour, and Lottie was clearly impatient, "I don't like waiting an hour to make cookies. Maybe I should have asked which one was faster, not easier."

I couldn't help but let out a small laugh, "I know. The waiting isn't the most fun part." I stepped around her to leave the kitchen and she started to follow. "Just one second," I held my finger up to her, "I'll be right back."

I turned on my heel and opened the closet, rummaging through the boxes I'd stacked in front to hide the second surprise of the day. Finally, I found the small green bag I'd hidden in the back of the closet and returned to the kitchen.

"What's this?" Lottie touched her headband absentmindedly.

"Well, traditionally when you first learn about the cookies, you get to pick out your cookie cutter." I fiddled with the string on the bag, "But I wanted it to be a surprise, so I had to improvise." I handed her the bag and held my breath. She untied the bag and reached inside to pull out the Christmas tree cookie cutter I had chosen for her.

Her face gave nothing away so my nerves took over, "I hope it's okay."

"It's perfect," she turned it over in her hands. "Good thing I didn't pick gingerbread. Gingerbread trees aren't exactly traditional."

"In this family," I turned around and pulled my snowflake cookie cutter out of the drawer, "All shapes of gingerbread are welcome." I put on my most serious 'teacher giving a lecture' face and stared at her.

"Okay," she stood up on her toes to kiss my forehead. "But I'm still glad my trees get to be sugar cookies."

I shook my head, "Good, because that's what we made."

"Can we make them yet?" she crossed her arms and slowly edged towards the fridge.

"It's only been fifty minutes," I pointed to the clock on the microwave. "And the recipe says at least an hour."

She pouted and opened the fridge. "Please?"

"Oh, fine. But if it goes wrong, you aren't blaming me."

She looked up towards the ceiling for a split second before replying, "Okay. That sounds fair."

I couldn't help but smile, seeing her have this much fun, and I was powerless to resist her request. Instead of telling her all of that, all I said was, "A good sous chef does what he's told." Then I pulled the dough out of the fridge and put it down on the counter in front of Lottie.

She looked at the lump of dough in front of her, "So, how am I supposed to do this?"

"Well, first you take off the plastic," I joked, handing her the rolling pin. "And then you use a rolling pin and you just kind of roll until it's thin and flat."

She unwrapped the dough and picked it up, ready to transfer it to the counter.

"Wait!" I held my hand up, "first we have to put flour on the counter." I pulled some flour out of the bag and flicked it onto the counter, but some of it went flying off and hit Lottie square in the face. I winced, "Oh, I'm sorry." I was trying really hard not to laugh, but it wasn't working. A few bursts of laughter escaped my lips.

Slapping the dough down on the counter, she put her hands on her hips and looked at me through narrowed eyes, "You did that on purpose, Mister." She brushed the flour off of her face.

I held my hands up in defense, "I didn't. I swear."

She took one sudden step towards me, causing me to jump backward and use my arms to protect my face. Lottie was apparently satisfied with scaring me because she returned to her dough, deciding not to retaliate for the flour incident. At least for now.

CHAPTER 12

Charlotte Sweet

I was covered from head to toe in flour, but I didn't care one bit. It was worth it to have this experience with Eli. I felt like I was on Cloud 9, experiencing what a childhood should look like for the first time. Eli said, *making cookies is a right of passage* and at first I was skeptical but I now had a new love for baking. Rolling out the dough was satisfying as it slowly turned into a flat oval.

I turned to Eli, showing him the final product. "How's that?"

He smiled and gave me a thumbs up. I reached over and took the christmas tree shaped cookie cutter in my hand. It lingered over the freshly rolled dough. Anxiety rose in my chest as I worried about messing it up. After so much work I had high hopes for these cookies.

"What now?" I asked, prolonging making the first cut.

"Now we find an edge," he said, pointing at one side of the dough, "and make the first tree." He reached his hand out and positioned my hand and the cookie cutter just above the spot he was pointing to. "Just press down."

I took in a shaky breath and made contact with the dough. I pressed down hard before I removed the cookie cutter, seeing the outline of a tree. Once I got a feel for what I was doing, I continued until the whole surface was covered in tiny christmas trees. Eli's hand lingered on the small of my back as he stepped closer, so close that I could feel his breath against my neck.

It was a taste of the life I always wanted. Even though I wasn't really a part of his family, somehow I still felt like I was. Everyone was just so nice and welcoming. I knew that I would have to let it all go when my car was done. It couldn't last forever because of one fact. We weren't family. My family was somewhere out there, waiting for me to find them.

Eli's voice broke me from my thoughts.

"Are you all right?" He smiled, his eyes searching mine. "It looks good." He carefully pulled the excess dough from around the trees and put it to the side. "We can just pick them up and put them up on the tray," he said when I didn't answer him.

I nodded and started to peel each individual tree off the counter carefully. Eli sighed and helped lay them down on the cookie sheet. Twelve perfect cookies. I slid on a pair of oven mitts and put the tray in. "How long do they go in for?"

"Try ten minutes, for now." He was still looking at me, and it seemed like he wanted to ask me more, but he just shook his head and set the timer.

I pulled myself up onto the counter. "Now we wait."

He began cleaning the counter. "Yeah, now we wait."

As he wet a cloth and began to wipe down the countertops, every now and then he would glance back at me. His forehead was creased as if deep in thought and it didn't take a genius to know what he was thinking about. My past was mysterious and even though I wanted it to stay that way, part of me felt like he deserved to know because I was about to put him through hell.

"My um, my mom gave me up for adoption when I was a baby, although I wasn't adopted right away because of some health issues, which are all sorted now, but it was why I was placed in foster care," I began. Eli slowly turned to face me, his expression softening as I spoke. "So from the age of two until I turned eighteen, I was in eight different foster homes. Some were okay and some were horrible, but I just never felt like part of the family, you know?"

I gulped, hesitating before continuing. Eli stepped toward me, placing his hands gently on my knees as my legs swung off the counter.

"When I aged out of the system, I didn't have anywhere to go, so I started living out of my car, which was all I could afford after working for years. It was okay for a while, but I knew I wouldn't last the winter. My social worker had given me some information on my birth family since I was considered an adult and could receive it from the court. I was on my way to find my birth mother when I got stuck." I huffed and waited for Eli to say something, anything. "And here we are."

He was staring at me, frozen except for his hands drawing circles on my knees. "I don't-" he said, dropping his eyes to stare at his hands. "I didn't know that. I just-"

I pursed my lips together, feeling my emotions rush to the surface. I wasn't sure why it was so hard to talk about, it was just my life, not a tragedy. Though, with each second that passed, I was closer and closer to tears. Maybe that was what I was so afraid of. Showing Eli my weaknesses.

When he looked back up at me, his eyes were also glistening with tears. "I had no idea, Lottie. I can't imagine how hard that must have been for you. I'm so sorry." He reached his hand up and brushed the tear from my cheek. "You deserve to find your family."

I lifted my hand and ran my fingers through his hair, finding the back of his neck. Pulling him closer, I laid my forehead gently against his. He always knew what to say and it meant so much to me. Even if I wasn't sure that it was true. He inched toward me and cupped my cheeks, kissing my lips. It sent a tingling feeling down my spine as I deepened the kiss, pulling him even closer.

"Thank you," I whispered as we broke apart. "For making me feel like I could tell you that."

Just then the timer went off, sending an irritating beeping through the kitchen. Eli cleared his throat and opened the oven, checking on our creation. I peered in seeing a light brown line around each of the cookies. A frown pulled at my lips. "They're overdone, aren't they?"

He poked at the edge of one of them. "Yeah, a little bit. But we can rescue them with some icing once they cool."

Eli pulled out the tray and laid it on the stove top as he examined the cookies. He seemed unphased by their appearance, so it eased my disappointment. I wrapped my arms around his waist, burying into his side. My frown was replaced by a smile as I felt him kiss the top of my head. "Oh icing!"

"You're cute," he cooed and latched onto my hand. Slowly he pulled me into the living room, his eyes not leaving mine for a second.

My mind wandered, thinking we were about to make out on the couch like a scene from the movies. Instead, Eli sat me down seeming like he wanted to talk but about what? There were several heavy topics hanging over our heads to choose from.

He sat down beside me, just close enough to take both my hands in his. He opened his mouth to speak and then sighed. "I don't want to make you feel uncomfortable, Lottie. So just tell me if I'm way off base, okay?" He scooted a little closer and his knee brushed mine.

I nodded, thinking about my words. I wanted to say the right thing. "It's okay, I'll let you know if it's too much. Ask away."

"Will you tell me a little bit about living in foster homes? I know you said some were good and some weren't and I just..." he trailed off, gazing intensely into my eyes. "I want to understand."

"I did have some good experiences in foster care, don't get me wrong. It wasn't all bad, but it's hard to feel like you fit into an already complete family, especially when you know that it's not long term. Other's wanted to have a foster kid to babysit their young kids. Some were just..." I was at a loss for words. I didn't know how to explain it to him in a way he'd understand. From experience, only other foster kids really understood what it was like, but I had to try. "Abusive."

He winced, drawing back slightly, but keeping a firm grasp on my hands. His eyes were filled with anguish as he looked into mine. *What would make him look at me like that?*

"I-" he started, stopping to think before he continued. "I can't imagine how that was for you. I can't pretend to know what abuse is like. But I'm so, so sorry, Lottie. No child—no person—should have to live through that." He stopped to look out the window, and I thought he was done. I was about to respond when he turned back to face me.

"And Lottie?" He pulled me closer with his hands, inching closer to me as his eyes danced across my face. "No family is ever too complete to fit in someone new, do you hear me?"

I nodded, but my gaze fell to the floor. His thumb grazed my chin and tilted my head back up to look at him. His eyes pleaded with me to agree. "Okay, yeah I hear you and uh- don't be sorry, it's not your fault."

"I know." He tried to smile, but it didn't reach his eyes, they were full of something that seemed a lot like pity. "But you don't deserve that and I..." he trailed off. "I don't want you to feel like no one cares for you because-" he took a deep, shaky breath - "because it isn't true."

Tears pooled in my eyes and as they spilled over I quickly wiped them away. "Eli..." My voice hitched. "I care about you too, but we've only known each other for less than a week."

"Yeah, I... Of course." He pulled his hands out of mine and slunk back into the opposite corner of the couch, staring at his hands. "I shouldn't have said anything."

I bit down on my lip, kicking myself for hurting his feelings. Immediately I wanted to take it back and go back to the bliss we felt when we were making cookies. "It's not that, I just- I'm leaving soon Eli."

There was a long silence between us that filled the room. Finally he looked up at me, once again forcing the smile that didn't reach his eyes. "I know, Lottie. Think nothing of it. It's nice to have you here as long as you want to stay, but I'll get your car fixed up and you'll be off to find your family. It's a good thing."

"Yeah..." I agreed but deep down I was conflicted about leaving. The thought of leaving him made my heart ache. I'd let myself care and I was going to get my heartbroken.

"I think those cookies are probably cool now." He stood up and brushed the back of his hand across his eyes. "I'll just go get the stuff ready for the icing." He took a few steps and then turned around to face me. "Do you want to come?"

"Yeah, I'll come," I said and trailed close behind as he walked to the kitchen. Briefly, I squeezed my eyes shut, trying to banish the urge to reach out and fix things. But I was scared that even then, it wouldn't do any good. I couldn't abandon my dream of finding my family for him and our week of bliss. That would have been foolish. I just had to hope that he understood. "Eli?" his name slipped off my tongue and his eyes met mine. "I'm sorry."

"There's nothing to be sorry about." He looked at me, his eyes glinting as he smiled. "It isn't your fault." He reached down and took my hand, pulling me towards him. "Now, I believe we were about to ice some cookies. Can't have you missing a crucial element of the Christmas tradition."

A smile tugged at my lips. "Alright, let's do this."

CHAPTER 13

Cole Blackwood

I managed to push down all the complicated feelings from the night before as I drank my third cup of coffee on the road to drop Lottie off at work. She was dancing to whatever song was on the radio, as she always did. Something about what she told me the night before made me see her dancing in a different light, though. And I couldn't help but wonder if it was something she did to hide her pain or if she was genuinely happy here.

Is it wrong of me to hope it's the latter, not for her, but for myself? I parked my truck in front of the cafe and waited for the song to finish before I turned off the truck.

"Have you always done that?" I blurted out the question I'd been dying to ask for the whole trip to work, despite having planned to keep it inside. "I mean, have you always danced to whatever song came on the radio? You don't seem to have a preference. I l-" I stopped myself from saying 'love' and smiled to hide the nerves. "I like that you'll dance to whatever music I play."

She giggled before answering, "Force of habit I guess. I love to dance and in some of the foster homes I wasn't allowed to pick the music. If I waited for a song to come on that I liked, I'd never get the chance. So I decided I could make any song a dance song."

It wasn't the answer I was hoping for, but it sounded true. Finally getting her to tell me the truth had to count for something. "That makes sense," I replied when I noticed her staring at me. We were staring at each other, drawing closer with each breath. But we were interrupted by a knock on the window. I looked up to see my mom's face peering in as she waved.

"Can you roll down the window?" I asked Lottie. "I think my mom wants to talk to us."

Lottie did as I asked and as soon as the window was halfway down my mother made her reasoning clear. "I'm sorry to burst in like this, dear." She looked at Lottie. "I really need you in there for the breakfast rush."

"Oh." Lottie looked back at me before turning back to my mom. "I'll come right in. Of course."

"Bye, Lottie," I said, waving as she stepped out of the car. I adjusted the heat down as she left the truck, but the door didn't shut behind her. I looked up, thinking she wanted to say something, but I saw my mother standing in the doorway, climbing into the passenger seat.

"What are you doing?" I asked as she closed the door behind her.

"I just wanted to have a chat with my son," she said, crossing her arms across her chest.

"Mmmhmm." I'd been her son long enough to know that was never the case. "So what is it actually?" I asked.

"I just wanted to talk to you and see how everything is going. I noticed Lottie's still around and I thought that was temporary. Do you know how long she'll be staying?"

Did she bug my apartment or something? I tried to figure out what she was getting at, but her face was stoic. As usual, she gave nothing away.

"No, I don't know how long she'll be staying," I tried to keep my voice level, but my emotions slipped out at the end, betraying me.

"I thought so." She smiled and put her hand on my elbow. "I'm just an old lady who happens to be your mother," she launched into something resembling her usual speech. "But I think maybe you should talk to

Lottie about when she's planning to leave. If she's going to be staying around for a while, I'd like to have her over again."

"Mom, I already said I don't know when she's leaving."

"I heard you, son." She paused to assess my face. "That's what I'm worried about. You two are getting awfully close."

"Can you just say what you're trying to say, Mom? I have to get to work before I'm late." I pointed at the clock on the dashboard for emphasis, though I was sure I was already late.

"I don't want to see you get hurt, Cole. And I don't want to see Lottie get hurt either." She waited for me to say something, but I just stared at my hands on the steering wheel.

"You've both been spending a lot of time together. If she's going to leave, it might be best you act accordingly."

"Thanks, Mom." I couldn't help the sadness from spilling over into my words. No matter how much I wanted her to be wrong. I knew she was right.

As she always did when she knew I'd understood her message, she changed the subject. "So, are you going to be able to come by for supper one of these days before Lottie leaves? We'd really love to see her again."

I smiled. "I don't see why not, Mom. I'll have to ask Lottie, though."

She nodded and popped open the door. "Take care of yourself, Cole."

When she slammed the door it shook the whole truck, and I watched her jog back into the cafe. As the door opened, I caught a glimpse of Lottie, hair tied up behind her and looking as beautiful as anyone I'd ever seen. Maybe more.

Shit!

I slid the truck into gear and drove a little faster than was legal, trying to get to work on time. I raced out of my truck and through the back garage door mere seconds before I was supposed to start work.

"I'm sorry!" I called out to Joe as soon as I was inside. "I had to drop Lottie off at the diner and my mom decided it was a good time for some motherly advice."

"Just get to work, Eli," Joe called back from his office. "I don't pay you to tell me about your mother's advice."

I got changed and grabbed the schedule for today. There were a lot of small jobs, as usual. I spent the whole morning thinking about Lottie and performing mundane tasks like tire rotations and fluid checks. I couldn't get her out of my head. Everything I tried to think about somehow circled back to her face when she told me we didn't know each other well enough. *Maybe she's right,* the small voice in my head told me.

And maybe she was, but I couldn't shake the feeling that I did know Lottie. I knew her at least enough to know that I wanted her to stay. I knew myself well enough to know that it would tear me apart if she left.

"Hey!" Joe stuck his head under the truck I was working on. "Are you alive down there or what?"

"Sorry, Joe." I shook my head to clear it. "I was just distracted."

"A lot of that going around with you, lately," he muttered to himself. "I was just going to say it's time for lunch. Go have a sandwich or something."

I got out from under the truck and stood up. Watching his back disappear around the corner of his office, I couldn't help but laugh. The man knew how to make an exit.

I washed my hands and ran back to my truck to get my lunch, not bothering to remove my overalls. When I came back in carrying my lunch, Joe called me over again.

"I forgot to tell you," he said, beckoning me into his office. "This box arrived for you with the mail this morning. Looks like the part you've been waiting on."

My heart sank and my stomach twisted into a knot. *That's it, then. I have a day and then she's gone.*

"Eli?" Joe waved his hand in front of my face. "Are you feeling okay? Maybe you should go home."

"No, no. I'm fine," I lied. "I just spaced out for a minute." I shook my head again. "I'll just go grab the box from your office and make sure it's what we think it is," I said, more to console myself than answer him. He took it as an answer anyway and sat down to his lunch.

The box was barely open and it was clear it was Lottie's part. I pushed it back into the box and threw it onto a shelf and Joe's eyes suspiciously followed me around the shop for the rest of the afternoon.

Around 3:30, as we were getting ready for the last appointment of the day, Joe handed me my coat.

"Go home, Eli," he said. "And come back tomorrow ready to work, please."

"I don't need to go home," I protested. "I'm fine, just a little distracted."

"I don't have any more work for you to do."

I knew he was lying, because there was always work to do. "Okay," I drew the word out like a question, "If you're sure."

"I am sure. Now go home and I'll schedule some time for you to work on that Lottie's car tomorrow afternoon."

"Thanks," I said, though I wished more than anything that he wouldn't. I was desperately searching for a reason not to fix her car—to give me more time with her.

I wracked my brain the whole way to my truck and the whole drive to the diner. *How am I going to keep her here?* was an almost constant refrain.

But once I was parked in front of that cafe, watching Lottie's smile light up the whole room, I knew there was no way I could do that. It was one thing to hope she chose to stay, and entirely another to force her to. And no matter which way I carved it, I didn't want her to have to stay, I wanted her to *want* to.

So I did the only thing there was to do: I took off my seatbelt, hopped out of the truck, and walked straight into the diner to meet Lottie. When the bell over the door signaled my arrival, it felt like the whole room turned to face me, but it was Lottie's eyes I searched for.

"Hey!" she waved, her smile shining brightly across the room. "I'll just be a few minutes, okay?"

I couldn't speak through the lump in my throat, so I just nodded and made my way over to an empty table to wait for her. It wasn't even two minutes later when she sat down in front of me and slumped her chin into her hand.

"Sorry about the wait," she said, brushing a stray hair out of her face. "I had to finish up my last table. And I wasn't expecting you here quite so early."

"Yeah." I took a deep breath and looked her straight in the eyes. "I have some good news, though!" I tried to sound enthusiastic, though her skeptical response made me question my success.

"The part for your car came in," I said, letting my eyes drift towards the table so I didn't have to see her excited expression. "I should be able to work on it tomorrow or the next day and get you on the road again."

CHAPTER 14

Charlotte Sweet

My heart sunk at the news that the part was in for my car. It felt too early. I thought I had more time to spend here with Eli. Once it was fixed I'd have no excuse to stay, I'd have to continue my journey to find my birth mother and say goodbye to these lovely people. I didn't let my disappointment show on my face, instead, I nodded and forced myself to smile.

"That's great," I lied through gritted teeth. My hand grazed over his arm as I turned away and headed toward the door, finally letting my smile fall. Eli trailed close behind, so close I could feel his warmth.

A sigh escaped his lips and his hand wrapped around my arm, turning me back to face him. His eyes searched mine, like he was hoping to understand. He took a deep breath and slid his hand down until it was holding mine. "Hey, my mom wants to know if we'll go over there for dinner tonight. I should probably answer her before we leave." His fingers squeezed my hand ever so gently before he finished. "So, do you want to go?"

He patiently waited for my reply, although it didn't take me long to make my decision. I had to go on like everything was okay. Maybe if I tried hard enough then it would be. "Yeah, sure. Let's go over for dinner. I don't mind."

His smile widened and he stepped towards me before abruptly pulling back and rubbing the back of his neck. "I'll... I'll go tell my mom then, okay? You want to wait here or out in the truck?"

"I'll wait here," I said and let go of his hand, giving him a gentle push toward his mother who was finishing up counting the cash in the register.

He huffed and scuffed his foot against the tile floor before walking over to his mother. I watched a bright smile come to her face as Eli told her the news and she kissed his cheek. His words echoed in my head, *no family is ever too complete to fit in someone new.* I bit down on my lip to stop the tears from streaming down my face. Deep down I wished that this was my family.

Eli backed away from his mom and gave her a small wave. She in turn looked past Eli and waved excitedly at me. I smiled, feeling my heart ache in my chest. "Good to go?" I asked Eli as he stopped in front of me.

"Yeah, all good." He smiled and pushed the door open, letting a burst of cold air into the cafe. "I think she's probably going to make us eat our weight in food tonight, though. She's really excited about you coming for dinner."

I nudged his shoulder and chuckled. "I'm excited to eat my weight in food."

He laughed and pulled his jacket tighter around his neck. "You might not be once you actually try it. Mom's food is delicious, but there's way too much of it. Last time you got off easier, because she

"Oh really? I guess we'll see then if I can move tomorrow," I joked trying to ease the tension between us. The news of the part being in for my car put a damper on my mood and he seemed off as well. Maybe we were both trying to pretend like it was nothing, either way, I wanted things to go back to normal between us.

He cleared his throat, walked around the truck and opened the door. He looked back to see me frozen in place on the sidewalk. "Are you coming?" he asked, pulling himself up and into the truck.

"Yeah, sorry," I quickly covered and hopped in, hoping he didn't notice how lost in thought I was. Typically I was better at hiding how I truly felt. Around him though, it was harder. It felt like I was lying and I cared too much about him to lie.

❄❄❄

Eli parked the truck in his parents' driveway but didn't get out of the car. His shoulders shrugged dramatically as he took the key out of the ignition. I couldn't peel my eyes away, no matter how scared I was that he would notice I was starring. His mouth opened but closed again, as if he was about to say something and decided against it. It was my turn to break our silence.

"Should we go in?" I asked, my voice a mere squeak. I wanted to kick myself for sounding so meek. He turned toward me and placed a hand on my knee. With one touch, the tension floated away. For me at least. For him the crease on his forehead said otherwise. "You know, this is my best Christmas yet," I said and pushed my hand against his shoulder.

"It's not Christmas yet!" His smile brightened and he brushed a small piece of hair out of my face. "I still have time to make this Christmas even better." He turned away from me too fast to tell if he was okay about all of this, but I opened the door, hopped out of the truck and followed him into the house.

"Hey, Mom!" he called after closing the door behind us.

Jan scurried out from the kitchen, her arms open wide to pull her son into a hug even though she'd just seen him an hour earlier. "You're just on time, dinner is almost ready." She turned to me and cupped my cheek with the palm of her hand. "I'm so glad you came."

"Me too, Jan," I replied.

She quickly turned back to her son and swatted him with the dish towel that was slung over her shoulder. "Be a gentleman and take her jacket, I will check on dinner."

"Oh, of course." He stepped around behind me and his hands brushed my shoulders as he gripped the upper edge of my coat. Jan walked back to the kitchen, leaving us to fend for ourselves. "May I take your coat, Lottie?"

I giggled as he asked permission. "Of course, silly." He stepped away, hanging my jacket up in the closet but quickly came back to my side. I reached forward, swinging our fingers as the smell of a freshly cooked meal wafted into the hall. "I wonder what's for dinner. It smells amazing."

Eli stepped forward and tugged on my hand, guiding me into the kitchen. His dad was sitting at the bar, drinking a glass of red white while reading the newspaper as Jan pulled a casserole out of the oven. As she turned around her eyes landed on our joined hands. Immediately, I felt warmth rush to my cheeks. I swung my hand loose and laid it on my hip as naturally as possible.

"Is there anything I can do to help, Jan?" I asked.

"If you and Eli wouldn't mind setting the table, that would be very helpful," she suggested.

"Yeah of course." I said but Eli had already stepped into the kitchen to collect the silverware. He didn't wait for me, instead, he started toward the dining room with all the supplies in hand. I bit down on my lip, feeling as though I'd done something wrong. "Eli?" I asked, hesitantly when we were alone.

"Yeah?" he looked up from what he was doing to look at me.

"Everything okay?" My heart pounded in anticipation of his answer.

"Yeah, it's okay," he replied, fiddling with the cutlery he had already set. "Actually..." I pursed my lips and tried to swallow down my anxiety. I balled my hands into fists and told myself not to panic as I waited for him to continue.

"Actually, can I ask you something?" He sat down on the chair and looked at me, waiting for me to say it was okay. I sat down beside him and nodded, accepting the hand he reached out for me and lacing our fingers together again.

He looked at our hands and smiled at them, using his free hand to draw circles on the back of my hand. "I was just wondering why... before ... why you ..." He looked down at our hands again and I could feel his fingers squeeze mine ever so slightly. After one more deep breath, he found the words. "I was wondering why you pulled apart from me so quickly earlier. I thought..." He shook his head and looked anywhere but my face.

"I'm sorry," I muttered and looked down at our hands. "I guess I just got scared, I don't know what your mom thinks of- this- us, and I panicked. Maybe she thinks I'm not..." I trailed off, suddenly feeling selfish. "I'm not good enough for you."

"For me," he repeated, so low I almost couldn't hear it. His smile reached his eyes as he lifted our clasped hands to his lips and kissed the back of my hand. "How about you let me worry about my mother, okay? She wouldn't have asked you to be here if she didn't love you already."

I nodded. "Yeah, you're probably right."

"So can we say we'll focus on having a good time and not worry about what my mother thinks?" He stood up and pulled me up with him. Instead of answering, I embraced him, throwing my arms around his neck. Eli stepped back, catching my weight and returned the hug. The tension that had been between us drifted away and a genuine smile crept onto my lips.

The sound of someone clearing their throat behind us made my heart jump. Eli's arms fell to his sides as I turned to face Jan. She placed the salad bowl on the table and examined our setting job. After fixing a few crooked knives, she announced, "Come dish up your dinner. Don't want it getting cold now do we?"

She sent Eli a wink as she exited the room. He held out his hand to me and I locked my fingers through his. It felt like a bold gesture, declaring our unspoken relationship to his parents. Although, as we walked into the kitchen, neither his mom nor dad mentioned it. I was thankful for that, otherwise it would have been a very awkward dinner.

The meal Jan made was delicious. The kind of freshly cooked dinner that made me go back for seconds, and Eli thirds. If there was one thing he was right about, it was that Jan made more than enough. I was stuffed.

"Why don't us girls clean up? Wasn't there something you wanted Cole to take a look at Robert?" Jan said as she collected our now empty plates.

"Oh that's right. The car was making a strange noise so who better to look at it than our mechanic son?" Robert laughed and clapped a hand against Eli's back.

Eli looked at me and then back to Robert. "Yeah, sure Dad. I'll come take a look."

"Good." Robert stood up and clapped Eli on the back once again. "It's out in the garage. I'll come with you."

Eli gave me one last glance, his hand lingering against the wall before he followed his dad to the garage. Dishes clinked together as Jan began to clean up. I heaved a sigh and stood, lending a helping hand although I'd never been much good at doing the dishes. After collecting a few plates, I carried them to the kitchen sink and turned on the water.

"Oh dear, you don't have to do that. That's what the dishwasher is for." Jan laughed and pointed to the white appliance next to me. I giggled, covering over my embarrassment. She opened the top and began to load the dishes into the dishwasher. Clapping her hands together, she looked to the empty casserole dish and the several pots still sitting on the stove. "I can take care of those later. Right now, I thought it'd be nice if you and I had a little chat."

Jan pulled herself up onto one of the barstools and tapped the one next to her. Hesitantly, I sat down and tried to remember what Eli said. *She wouldn't have asked you to be here if she didn't love you already.* It didn't give me much peace of mind though.

"I've loved spending time with you dear, you're a lovely young woman. I think we have a lot in common, you see I didn't have an easy past either before I met Robert," she started, although I was expecting a "*but*" to follow. "How long will you be staying?"

There it was, just worded differently. *She's just worried for her son,* I told myself. "Eli got the part in for my car today, so it shouldn't be long before I'm able to get back on the road." I chose my words carefully, but that didn't stop her smile from falling. "I hope that I'd be welcome to come back though, I really like it here and..."

"Yes dear?" She urged me to continue.

I took a deep breath. "And I'm falling for your son."

CHAPTER 15

Cole Blackwood

I sat in my truck after a long day of work, during which I'd managed to do precisely one thing: fix Lottie's car. I'd spent nearly every moment of the last day with Lottie's words ringing through my head. *I'm falling for your son.* I should have gone to her right then and asked her to stay. I should have done something—anything—to keep her with me.

But instead, I was sitting in my truck spinning her keys in my hands and debating what I was going to do. The right thing to do would be to hand over her keys and let her go. But every time I thought of that, my heart knotted in my chest. *How do I let her go?*

My phone chimed with the alert I'd set to make sure I picked Lottie up on time. I drove as slowly as possible, giving myself as long as possible to prepare myself for the eventual conversation. I took the whole five minutes steeling myself to tell her that her car was ready. *I have to let her go.*

I parked the truck in front of the diner and took a deep breath. After throwing Lottie's keys into my pocket, I jogged through the increasing snow storm and opened the door to the cafe.

"Oh my!" Lottie ran up to me and wrapped her hands around my neck. "I thought you might be stuck somewhere. I was worried, but your mom said to just wait and... Hi," she said, reaching up and placing a kiss on my cheek. My skin warmed where she touched and her cheeks turned a vibrant red. I slid my thumb across her cheek and pulled her up towards me, placing a small kiss on her forehead as she hugged me. *I can't let her go.*

"What do you say we have a..." I swallowed my fear. "What do you think about going on a date? With me. Tonight." I kissed her again, not ready to see her response just then. Finally, she pushed me off her and stared up at me, the biggest sparkle in her eye as her mouth spread into a wide smile.

"I'd say let's go!" she giggled and pulled me over to the staff room so she could grab her coat and purse. As she kept reminding me, we hadn't known each other very long. But that wasn't stopping me from feeling drawn to her more strongly with every passing moment.

"I'm ready!" she said, smiling and holding out her hand. 'Where are we going?"

She had become so much brighter since I'd met her. I wanted to let myself believe it was because of me. "Sorry," I said when I noticed her smile wane slightly, "I was thinking of a surprise."

I felt my breath hitch in my chest as her smile returned and she nodded, pulling herself closer into my arms.

"Bye, Mom!" I called as I held the door open for Lottie. "See you!"

"Goodbye, Dear," Mom said, wiping her hands off on her apron.

When we stepped through the door, I pulled my zipper up on my jacket and ran towards the truck, pulling a scarf and toque out of the back. Lottie was halfway into the passenger seat when I noticed. "We aren't driving," I called to her. "I'm taking you somewhere close. Just grab your scarf and we'll go."

She eyed me through the back window, hesitated for a moment, and then climbed out of the truck. I wrapped my scarf around my neck and put on my mittens before sliding one of my arms around Lottie's shoulder.

"Have to make sure you stay warm," I said when she looked up at me.

"Yeah, okay," she replied, rolling her eyes. But she didn't make a move to escape my embrace, so I pulled her into my side as we walked down Main Street towards the park.

"Is it always this cold here?" she asked a block later, as I guided her into the park.

"No." I shook my head. "But it's always cold in the winter."

She laughed and tucked her head into my shoulder as we walked along the path that was twinkling with Christmas lights, interrupted occasionally by some type of holiday figurine.

"Who is that?" Lottie asked, when we finally reached Grimso the Elf.

"Oh I wish my dad were here to tell you, because he's way better at it that I am, but I'll try." I cleared my throat and pulled her along to keep walking. "Well, he's basically this huge town legend. I'm pretty sure my dad made him up just to keep us indoors on Christmas eve, though."

"Well that can't be the legend," Lottie looked appalled as she stepped away from me. "What is the poor elf known for?"

I laughed as she shivered and returned to the warmth of my arms. "Well, supposedly, when children open the doors or windows to their houses, the little elf Grimso sneaks inside and takes one of their presents."

Her laughter came out something like a snort and I couldn't help but join her.

"I know." I shook my head. "It's totally ridiculous. That's why I'm saying I think my dad made it up."

"That I believe," she giggled. "I'll have to ask him about it sometime."

I'll have to ask him about it sometime.

I'm falling for your son.

Her words rang in my head as we rounded the last corner of the path. I knew I was clinging onto every last hope she might stay, and I was pulling out all the stops for a date that might make her decision easier.

As soon as the lights of the rink were visible through the trees, I could feel Lottie practically bouncing with excitement. I looked down to kiss her cheek, but the look on her face wasn't entirely excitement.

"What's wrong?" I asked.

She bit her lip and looked up at me. "I've never skated before. But it's just a perfect Christmas experience, so I wanted to try. If you don't mind cutting our walk short, I mean."

No matter what I had planned, the look on her face would have convinced me to stay and skate with her. If there was one thing that would keep her here it was that perfect Christmas experience she'd been searching for.

"Yes," I said, unable to keep the smile off my face as the snowflakes collected in her hair. "Let's go skating."

It didn't take long to rent skates. And once I'd helped her tie them on properly, she stood up and took a few wobbly steps towards me.

"Whoa," she said, wobbling a little and clinging to my jacket with her gloved hands. "Why are these things so unbalanced?"

I laughed and pulled her onto the ice. "Probably as a form of torture," I laughed, skating backwards to bring her out until we were standing on the clear ice.

We stood there, staring at each other as people skated past us. If it weren't for the little guy barrelling towards us with his chair, I think we might have stayed there forever.

"Sorry, Eli!" Mrs. Jackson said as she pulled Simon out from under us. "He's just learning."

I opened my mouth to say 'it's okay' but Lottie beat me to it.

"It's all right." She smiled at Mrs. Jackson and Simon in turn. "I'm just learning, too."

Once Simon skated off with his chair and his mother, I gently pulled on Lottie's arms, skating backwards and dragging her along behind me.

"Keep your feet closer together," I instructed, trying to keep her from doing the splits on the ice. She snapped her feet together and almost fell over. "No. Like shoulder width apart."

She looked down at her feet as I began pulling her again, bending her knees and keeping her feet a good distance apart.

"Like this?"

"Yes." I let go of one of her hands and spun around so we were facing the same way. *No sense not showing off at all.* Tugging on her hand, I pushed her in front of me and then put my hands on either side of her waist.

"What now?" she said, focusing on the people in front of us and leaning to avoid collisions.

"Now, you just push from one foot to the other kind of?"

She laughed. "That's not very helpful."

"Sorry." I pushed her forwards and then let go, staying close by to catch her when she fell.

"I think I'll figure it out." She smiled back at me. "But will you hold my hand to keep me from falling?" She held her hand out for me to hold, and I had to pull her into me in order to avoid hitting an old man I didn't recognize under all his outerwear.

"So..." I began as Lottie and I started skating.

"Yeah?" She didn't look up at me, focusing instead of moving herself forward.

"Well, I was just wondering... You don't have to answer, but I was just wondering how much you know about your birth family." Suddenly, she stopped skating and pulled me to a halt. *When did she learn to stop?* Her eyes were locked on the ground. I kicked myself, feeling as though I had overstepped.

She heaved a sigh. "Um, well I don't know much. The only thing that I really was given was my birth mother's name but I found her online. She has a family and a daughter who would be my half sister."

"How old is she?" I asked. "The sister, I mean."

"From the picture I saw she looked young, maybe five or six years old."

"Not much older than my niece, then." I was struggling to find a way to connect with her. "It could be nice having a younger sister, though."

"Yeah I think it would be, I love kids." She smiled and started to skate again.

She was far ahead of me before I finally snapped out of my thoughts and chased after her. When I finally caught her, she was smiling ear to ear.

"Are you sure you haven't skated before?" I asked her. "Were you just pulling my leg?"

She smiled and skated away, giggling as the snow fell around her, turning her red hair almost white. I must have followed her around that rink twenty more times before the snow started getting so thick it was hard to see the streetlights. *If this gets any worse, it might not be safe to drive. We should get home.*

"Hey, Lottie?" I called after her, "I think we should go." I held out my hand and waited while she skated back to me, gripping my hand in her own. I pulled her through the thinning crowd towards the edge of the rink where the benches were and stepped off the ice.

I turned around to face her and carefully pulled her arms towards me. "Just step towards me and into the snow," I coached. "It'll be fine."

The next thing I know, Lottie's toe pick had caught on something and she crashed into me, sending us both flying to the ground in a puff of fresh powder. Her face was an inch from mine and all I wanted to do was kiss her. I put my hand up behind her head, drawing her closer to me.

"I told you I didn't know how to skate," was the last thing she said before closing the small space between us and kissing me. I let my hand slide into her hair while the other wrapped around her back, pulling her closer to me.

I definitely can't let her go.

CHAPTER 16

Charlotte Sweet

It felt I had a permanent smile on my face. As long as I was with Eli, it would never disappear. My heart felt complete, with all of these new experiences under my belt. The impending possibility of leaving kept trying to creep its way into my mind, but I wasn't going to let it. Forgetting was okay, for one night at least.

The whole drive home, Eli's hand was intertwined with mine as he navigated through the heavy snow. After parking in the driveway, he only let go briefly to get out of the truck. Wind slapped me in the face as I jumped out and my feet sunk into what looked like a foot of snow. Eli wrapped an arm around my waist. "Let's get inside!" he shouted over the howling wind.

I could barely see, but thankfully I didn't need to with him guiding me. I had never seen weather like this and even though it probably created a picture perfect morning, it was terrifying. Just the short walk made my face feel frost bitten. Eli slammed the door shut behind us and took off his gloves, rubbing his hands over mine to warm them up. He reached over and felt his way up the wall until he found the light switch.

I heard the familiar click, but instead of being welcomed by light, we remained in the dark. My eyes were quick to adjust, although it didn't solve the mystery. He tried again, but still no light.

"Ah, crap!" he muttered under his breath. "Power's out. Let me just go flip the breaker."

Without hesitating he rushed down the stairs and disappeared from view. Even though we were inside it still seemed chilly. After slipping out of my jacket, I laid it down on the bench beside the door. I expected the lights to turn back on momentarily, but after several minutes went by there was still nothing. Carefully, I made my way down the stairs.

"Eli?" I called out.

"One second," he called back from the utility room, his voice hoarse.

A few moments later, he returned, able to see me in the darkness now that his eyes were adjusted to the darkness of the basement. "It wasn't the breaker," he said when he reached me. "I think the power must be out because of this storm." He dropped his head a little and fiddled with my hand held in his own.

It was like someone had flipped a switch on his emotions along with the lights. Disappointment was written all over his body, even in the way his shoulders slumped toward me. Somehow, being in the dark didn't bother me. Making something from nothing was what I was good at.

"Do you have any candles?" I asked as I reached up and placed my hand on his bicep.

A smile spread across his face. "I do!" He slid his hand along the wall, guiding himself back to the utility room and returning with a box of candles. "I'm sorry in advance," he said as soon as he saw my face. "They're my mom's leftovers. She kept saying I needed some for emergencies."

I giggled. "As long as they light, that's what matters."

Eli handed me the box and took off the top. A collection of mismatched candles was inside, all of different shapes and sizes. I arranged them on the kitchen table and turned back to him.

I laid my fist against his chest and tugged at his sweater. "Do you have a lighter or some matches?"

"Umm..." he looked around and patted his pockets. "I don't know if I do, actually."

"Don't tell me you don't barbeque," I said and nudged his shoulder, playfully. "There's got to be a lighter somewhere."

"Oh!" His eyes brightened. "I do! It should be here somewhere." He rummaged through a drawer in the kitchen until he found what he was looking for. "Here it is," he said, putting it into my hand.

I stood on my tiptoes and kissed his cheek, ready to get our night started. "Thank you."

Eli watched me carefully as I littered the candles around the room, like I'd seen many times in romance movies. With each flame, the room took on a romantic atmosphere and damn, did Eli ever look good standing in the midst. His jaw bones were accentuated by the lights below. With one last candle, I returned to Eli's side where he stood in awe and set it down on the counter.

"How about we make a fire and get some blankets, camp out in the living room?" I took his hands in mine and smiled up at him.

He slid his hands around my back and pulled me towards him, hugging me as he kissed the top of my head. I heard him say something inaudible into my hair and pulled back to look at him with a raised eyebrow.

"I said yes," he said, smiling and pulling me back in for a hug.

My stomach grumbled, vibrating throughout the rest of my body. I prayed that Eli didn't hear, but his low chuckle told me otherwise. I gazed up at him, feeling a warmth creep up to my cheeks. "I'm kind of hungry, if you couldn't tell."

He shook his head and smiled. "I'll get us something to eat," he said, putting his hand on the door of the fridge.

When he paused, I asked him what was wrong.

"I'm just not sure what we have with the power out," he sighed and tapped his fingers against the fridge for a moment. "What do you say to sandwiches?" he asked, turning to face me.

Suddenly, I started to crave a certain type of sandwich that I hadn't had in a long time. My face lit up as I peaked around Eli and into the fridge. "Peanut butter and jelly?"

"I think I have some jelly." He rummaged around in the door of the fridge and then pulled it out triumphantly. "Yes! Let's make some sandwiches!"

Eli hopped in action and laid out all of the ingredients on the counter. He must have been hungry too, the way he rushed to get our five star meal ready. Either that or he was eager for what was coming later on in the night. Even though I was hungry, I took my time. I wanted this sandwich to taste like perfection. My mouth watered just thinking about the peanut buttery goodness.

Eli sent a shiver down my spine as he moved my hair to one side, his fingers grazing over my neck. He then snaked his arms around my waist and placed his lips against the skin where my neck met my shoulder. I slapped the two pieces of bread together and spun around in his grasp. "What are you doing?"

He kissed my nose and reached around me, picking up my sandwich. "Thanks for this," he said, immediately taking a huge bite. He grinned at me, holding the sandwich loosely in his hands, a glint in his eye.

I stood, my mouth ajar in shock as he chewed and swallowed a bite of my seemingly delicious sandwich because he proceeded to take another large chunk out of it. "Eli!" I cried out and snatched the sandwich out of his hand. The bread tore in half. As much as I wanted to be mad, I couldn't, the pout on his face was too cute but I couldn't let him get off so easy.

Folding my arms across my chest, I looked down at the floor. Apparently my look of disappointment was very convincing. Within seconds Eli wrapped his arms around me and rubbed my back gently.

"I can make you another one," he spoke softly and kept me wrapped in his arms. "I'll even make two. Will that make you feel better?"

I couldn't help but throw my cover out the window, giggling. "I'm just messing with you, it's fine. But I'd never turn down a sandwich made by you."

Eli rolled his eyes at me, but smiled. He moved back to the kitchen counter and quickly spread the peanut butter and jelly over two more sandwiches. I pulled myself up onto the stool and watched him work. He was so attentive as he set the scene. He placed our sandwiches down on the coffee table and turned on the fireplace. My eyes never left him, every movement. I got the feeling that he wanted things to be just as perfect as I did.

He took a handful of blankets out of the closet and threw them down on the couch. Although, one he set to the side before turning back to me.

"So..." He sat down on the couch, patting his hand on the seat beside him. "If you come here, you'll be warmer with the fireplace."

I closed the distance between us, my feet moving quickly beneath me. My heart pounded in anticipation of his touch and as I sat down I made sure my knee grazed against his. I bought my feet up on the couch and sat back, nudging his shoulder. Suddenly, he let out the fakest yawn I'd ever heard, starting at the top of the octave and working his way down as he stretched out his arms. *Ah, the ol' yawn and cuddle trick.* It had never been used on me before but the romance movies taught me a few things. I didn't mind though, it was beyond cute.

His arm wrapped around my shoulders and I leaned into him, feeling my heart settle. I felt at ease sitting in his arms. Now all we needed was a blanket to cuddle under. I shivered, rubbing my hands together making a *burrr* noise even though I wasn't cold.

Eli took the blanket off the armrest and laid it over our laps. It gave me an excuse to cuddle in closer. I slung my legs over his and snaked an arm around his waist.

Somehow, though I was practically glued to his side, Eli's hand reached for my shoulder and pulled me in even closer. He kissed the top of my head and then rested his cheek on my hair.

After three breaths — *not that I was counting* — he peppered my hair with more kisses and then sighed. "Lottie? Have you liked living here?"

I nodded into his chest. "Yeah, I think this is the best place I've ever lived."

"Even with working at the diner?" he asked me, loosening his grip on my shoulder ever so slightly. "Don't you ever feel like maybe you want more?"

"I don't think so, I mean, my life has been a rollercoaster of uncertainty where I had countless jobs to keep myself afloat. Here, there's none of that. It's... still. I like it," I trailed off, thinking that I probably sounded crazy but it was the truth.

"Me too," he said. "I mean, when I was younger I always imagined what it would be like to live in exciting big cities in other parts of the country. I even scared my mom by saying I was going to move to Spain one summer." He let out a low chuckle and turned his head to face me. "But in the end, I'm glad I stayed. I can't imagine a better place to live. You know, to grow old and... you know, live."

I heaved a heavy sigh and smiled, thinking about how his future looked. What I saw was a long and happy life here in Willowtree Valley, surrounded by family. "I wish I could grow old here."

"You could," he practically whispered. We sat in silence for a few moments, and when Eli finally spoke again his voice was upbeat and happy. "If you could pick whatever you wanted in the whole world, what would your ideal future look like?"

My eyes met his as the gears in my head spun, thinking of my perfect future. I bit my lip, wondering if it was too forward to say that it was here, with him. "Um..." I muttered, gathering my thoughts. "My future- well, I would live in a small town, like this one and have a stable job." *Say it Lottie!* My heart screamed. "And you'd be there."

I froze, waiting for his reaction.

"I would?" he asked, and I could see his brow furrow even in the dim light of the room. "I'd like that. I'd like that a lot." He smiled and then leaned down to place a slight kiss on my cheek. "I guess here is a pretty good place to live. I want to live somewhere with a lot of families, you know? Like where everyone just feels like family. All the kids running around the streets and coming to your house to borrow your football because theirs went over the fence..." he trailed off.

"That sounds really nice Eli," I said and placed my hand on his cheek. "I'd like that too."

Eli shifted so both of his hands were on my waist and pulled me closer. So close that our lips were seconds away from touching. His warm breath hit my cheek as I wrapped my arms around his neck. He crashed his lips against mine, tightening his grip around me. Every bone in my body ached for him to deepen the kiss, take it to the next level.

His tongue slid between my teeth and danced in my mouth until we were both out of breath. As we parted, I rested my forehead against his, breathing heavy. He was so unaware of the effect he had on me, it made me want to change my whole plan for him because here, I already had everything that I was searching for.

Damn, he's a good kisser, I thought to myself.

"You can say that again," he smiled at me. "I know it's true."

My breath hitched in my throat as I realized I'd said it out loud. Embarrassed, I covered my red cheeks with my hands. Eli chuckled and pulled my hands away from my face, entwining our fingers.

"And you, Lottie, are beautiful."

CHAPTER 17

Cole Blackwood

I spent the remainder of the evening staring at Lottie's face when I thought she wasn't looking and putting out more and more candles as the electricity refused to come back on. We talked about everything from tending fires, to our jobs, to my family. I noticed the clock above the fireplace read 10:30 when I finally decided to release Lottie from my arms.

"I should probably clean up the kitchen a bit," I explained when she looked up at me. Though I wasn't sure how much cleaning there was to do, I was desperately trying to occupy myself to assuage the nagging guilt that twisted my stomach into knots.

She'd be snowed in right now, anyway, I reasoned. But I knew it wasn't the whole truth. I owed her the whole truth. But every moment I spent with her little body resting on the side of my chest, the attachment to her grew stronger.

"You think the power will come back on tonight?" she asked, bringing me out of my thoughts.

"I don't know." I walked over to the window and picked up a candle so I could see out. "Looks like these windows are covered in snow. I can't tell if it's still snowing because the basement is buried under a snowbank."

Lottie's laugh rang through the house clear as a bell. I reached over to where she stood and pulled her in towards me, kissing her longer than I intended. When she pulled away from me, I looked down at my feet. "I'm sorry," I said without looking at her. "I didn't mean to shock you like that. I just..."

"Eli," she giggled. "Please don't apologize." And then she stood on her tiptoes and pulled my head down to meet hers, giving me a quick peck on the lips.

"Okay," I said, breathing in the smell of her as she hugged me. "I won't apologize."

"You have to stop doing that," she said, taking a step backwards and putting her hands on her hips, "or we'll never get anything done. I thought we had a kitchen to clean."

"Right," I said, following her into the kitchen where she was holding a butter knife and a plate.

"I don't think this will take too long. I don't even think we need two people to do this."

"Okay, give it to me," I said, reaching for the dishes. "Why don't you go get changed for bed?"

She froze to look at me, her eyes calculating as she looked me over. It seemed as though she was trying to decide how much a chance she had in a fight. "Okay, then." She handed me the knife and put the plate in the sink. "I will go, but I don't think I'm going to be warm enough, so you might have to help me find some layers."

She picked up a candle from the table and walked off down the hallway, looking back only once as she was almost out of view. "That doesn't look like dishes, Mr. Blackwood!" she teased, wagging her finger.

"I'll be done before you get back," I called after her. "I promise!"

It didn't even take me five minutes to clean the two dishes and return them to their places. I stood staring down the hallway and waiting for her return, but as five minutes turned to fifteen, I started to worry.

"Lottie!" I called, making my way down the hallway with the help of another candle. "Lottie, are you alright in there?"

"Yeah, I'm fine," came her muffled reply.

"You sure?" I stepped closer and stuck my ear to the door. It sounded like she was hopping around. "Because I don't want you burning anything down with that candle."

"I'll be right there!" she called, less muffled than before.

I left my ear pressed to the door, listening for any signs of distress, but none came. I was still there, leaning my head into the door, when Lottie opened it and I almost fell in on her.

"Look who's burning things down now," she giggled, catching my arm in her free hand. "I told you I was fine."

"Also," she said when we arrived back in the living room. "I was thinking I should maybe sleep near the fireplace to keep warm and make sure we don't burn the place down."

Damn this dim lighting! I can't see what her face looks like at all!

"I think that's a good idea," I said carefully. "I'll just go find all the spare blankets. You can have the couch and I'll sleep on the floor. Sound good?"

"Yeah," she said, sitting down on the couch. "I think that would be nice. I'm getting a little tired and I have work in the morning, so..."

Her tiny body moulded into the pillows in the corner of my couch and it took everything in me not to cuddle up beside her. Instead, I felt my way down the hallway to avoid using a candle around all those blankets. While I was there I threw on my pyjamas and brushed my teeth in the freezing water that came out of the tap.

When I got back to the living room, a pile of blankets in hand, Lottie was already asleep, head leaning against the side of the couch like a pillow.

"Lottie?" I asked, making sure she was asleep. "Lottie, I have blankets for you."

When she didn't answer, I dropped the blankets on the floor and gently pulled her until she was lying down on the couch. After blowing out all the candles and draping a few blankets over her, I pulled my own blankets into a pile on the floor about a foot away from the couch and threw down my pillow. I fell asleep looking at her peaceful face. I would wake up the next morning laying on the floor with her wrapped in my arms.

❄❄❄

I was just about to leave work the next day when Joe called me into his office.

"Yeah?" I asked, wiping my hands off on a rag and sliding out of my coveralls. "What's up?"

"I have the bill for your girl's car." He handed me an envelope. "I don't care who pays it, I'm still leaving the employee amount on there. Unless you want me to add your labour?"

I rolled my eyes and snatched the envelope from him. "No, Joe. That will be fine."

"I want it out of my shop, Eli. You can't put off telling her forever!"

Not wanting to listen to him, I slammed the shop door behind me and made my way to my truck. I pulled Lottie's keys out of my jacket pocket where they had been all day and dropped them into the cup holder in the center console.

I am going to tell her today, I decided. *And I am going to ask her to stay.* If I was being honest with myself, I wasn't sure I'd be brave enough on that second one. But I was determined to tell her the truth. They say if you love something, you have to let it go. But the thought of losing her is getting more and more unbearable by the day. I have to rip the bandaid off.

"Hey!" Lottie broke me from my thoughts as she opened the door to the truck. "You would not believe the day I've had."

"Why? What happened?"

I drove her home as she told me all about the antics of a group of young people who came in. We were already stopped in front of the house when she stopped.

"Why aren't we getting out?" she asked.

"I have to tell you something first."

"Okay?" she looked at me, her eyes searching mine for any sense of impending trouble.

"Oh, it's nothing bad!" I said, hoping to calm her nerves, though it felt like the news might bring the end of my comfortable world. I took a deep breath and pointed to the cup holder. "Your car is ready and we can go pick it up whenever you'd like."

"Really?" She looked down at the cup holder and gingerly picked up her keys. "It's all done?"

I nodded, unable to keep the sadness out of the smile I forced onto my face. "Yeah, it's all fixed up and ready to go. I fixed a few small things and replaced your windshield wipers and stuff so it should be good to go for a while." I looked down at my lap. "There might also be snow tires involved. But don't worry, if you come back through here in the summer, Joe will change them out for you. You won't have to pay for it. You don't even have to talk to me." I tried to joke that last part, but I was so nervous for her response that I just ended up awkwardly looking at my hands.

Lottie didn't say anything.

When I glanced up at her, she was twirling her keys around her finger and gazing out the window.

"I could take you to get it now if you'd like," I said, hoping she would say no.

"I guess that would be all right," she said after a moment. "But I don't think I need it just yet. We could always go tomorrow?" When her eyes met mine, they were full of hope.

"I mean, we did have plans to look at Christmas lights today, if you're still up for that?" I offered her the out and hoped she would grab on.

"Yeah," she said, nodding. "Exactly. I'm sure Joe wants my car out of the shop, though, so maybe I could pick it up tomorrow morning and then meet you back here after work?"

I smiled in spite of myself. "That would be perfect."

"And let me know what it costs, okay?" she asked as she opened the door. "I have money from the diner, so I'd like to pay for it."

"Joe's really slow with bills," I lied. "I'll make sure to get it tomorrow."

Hopefully that gives me enough time to figure out how to not make her pay for it.

"Okay, sounds good," she said, hopping out of the car and into about three feet of snowbank.

I couldn't help but chuckle as she shook her arms and legs around, hopping from one foot to the other and shouting, "Cold! Cold! Cold!" as she hopped toward the house. I helped her inside and sat on the couch thinking about the night before while she took a shower and got dressed.

Finally, probably an hour later, she emerged from my room dressed in the cutest outdoor ready outfit I'd ever seen.

"Where'd you get that?" I said, pointing to her hat. "It's really cute."

Cute? Is that what people say?

"Thanks." She gingerly reached up and adjusted the hat on her head, looking down as she did so. "I got it with a little of my diner money. Figured there was no reason to save it."

"I love it," I said honestly. "Are you ready to go look at lights?"

"Are you kidding?" She was practically bouncing. "Of course I am!"

"All right." I held out my hand for her and she took it. "Let's go get Christmasey! I'll buy you a hotdog when we get to the park."

"I can buy my own hotdog!" she protested.

"I know. But this is a date, right?" I waited for her response, not willing to breathe lest I disturb the fine balance of whatever relationship was between us.

"I guess it is." She smiled and a rosy pink blush coloured her cheeks just above her scarf.

"Good." I leaned down to kiss her cheek. "Then let's go."

CHAPTER 18

Charlotte Sweet

The cold air wisped around us, but I was too happy to care about getting frostbite. My fingers were toasty warm in my mittens, one even more so as it was fused with Eli's. It was crazy how much heat he gave off and I welcomed it with open arms, letting it radiate through me. The Christmas lights scattered perfectly over the houses were truly amazing. I knew now why Eli wanted me to see it.

I stared in awe at the reindeer that were suspended on the roof of someone's grand home. This was Christmas. This was magic. My heart was so full it felt like it could explode right there, my smile so wide that it physically hurt my cheeks. Though, what made it so special was the man standing beside me.

It felt like a dream. I still couldn't believe that he'd taken me in, asking nothing in return and gave me the Christmas of my dreams. If he'd let me, I'd stay here forever. Finding my birth mother was a pipe dream, but this was real. Could I really give that up? Did I even want to anymore?

My heart was torn, but I pushed it aside. One more night. That was tomorrow's problem.

"Oh Eli, this is just as amazing as you said and then some," I said under my breath, as the lights twinkled.

His eyes crinkled with his smile when he looked down at me. "I knew you'd love it." He followed my gaze to the giant blow up Santa upside down in someone's chimney. "That Santa's older than I am. He's kind of a big deal around here."

"Wow, that's crazy to me. People keep a blow up Santa longer than a child." I chuckled at the thought. How much care they must have given that silly blow up figure.

"Old Mr. Sanders is pretty serious about his Christmas decorations. I think his whole garage is basically a Santa repair shop at this point. But his wife used to take Christmas pretty seriously. I think he does it for her," he trailed off, but continued to watch me.

"That's sweet. Something to keep her spirit alive. I feel it, you know?" I met his gaze and smiled as we came to the next house. It was decorated from head to toe with lights of every color. Candy canes lined the driveway, twinkling while a Charlie Brown Christmas played on the projector. "What about this one?"

"Mr. Sanders would like that. You should tell him sometime," he said softly before gesturing to the house I had indicated. "And this... This is a bet that was lost." He laughed heartily at the story he hadn't told me yet.

"Guy who lives here, Ryan, went to school with me. He and a buddy were racing their cars on an old track outside of town—bad idea, by the way, I love cars but the place is a pit. Anyway, he bet he would beat his friend in a five lap race. Ended up stuck in a mud puddle. So, as a result, the kids at the school got to plan the decorations for Ryan here. As you can see, they had a really good time!"

If I thought I couldn't smile wider, I was wrong. "That's...awesome."

"Yeah, he's a good guy. Keeps us in business down at the shop, too, because he's got no skills fixing cars." He turned to face me as we stood in the middle of the road. This wouldn't have been possible in the city. Cars would have ran us down without thinking twice. Here, there wasn't a car to be found, except for the ones that were parked to look at the lights.

"Thank you for this, Eli," I muttered as my eyes flickered down to his lips.

"You're welcome." He took a step closer and wrapped his arms around my back. "I'm glad I got to show you."

I stood on my tiptoes, so we were so close I could feel his breath against my cheek. His hand trailed up my arm and sat at the nape of my neck. The gesture sent shivers down my spine as the urge to kiss him doubled by the second. As our lips touched, I made my decision. This was it. I was meant to be right here, with Eli, for the rest of my life. I knew right then, I loved him.

As we parted, both out of breath, I muttered, "It's perfect." All of the thoughts in my mind that were swirling around came out as those two little words.

"Yeah," Eli sighed. "A perfect last night. With Christmas lights and stars and maybe later some hot chocolate." He smoothed my hair down with his hand and kissed the top of my head.

My stomach churned as my thoughts began to spiral. Deep down I knew that he didn't say anything wrong, but for some reason it just made my heart ache. The reminder that this was my last night here, my last night with Eli was not welcomed. It brought tears to my eyes as I let my mind run wild. The fear that I'd never see him again was too much to bear. As his words echoed in my head, I couldn't help but wonder if it was his way of saying that he didn't want me around anymore.

Maybe I was nothing but a burden to him and his family. Maybe he was just too kind to tell me. My hands fell from his waist and I turned back toward the lights, the colors all melting together.

I forced myself to smile. "Yeah... perfect."

"You okay?" he asked. When I didn't respond he added, "What's wrong?"

I shrugged it off, trying to ignore the awful feeling in the pit of my stomach. "It's nothing. Everything's fine, Eli." Though, I couldn't meet his gaze as I crossed my arms over my chest. The cool air was beginning to seep in through my jacket.

"Well, I can tell it's not nothing," he started. *Curse his perception.* He turned me around to look in my eyes. "Is it about finding your family? Are you afraid you won't find them or something? Lottie, I'm—"

"I said, everything's fine!" I repeated, more harshly than I wanted. I bit my lip, trying to hide my guilt.

"Okay. It's fine then," he said, turning toward another nearby house. "And this is the Baylors'. As you can see they have a ... unique opinion about Christmas decorations." He swept his hand across the yard and my eyes didn't know what to take in first, but I welcomed the distraction.

On the front lawn were an insane amount of blow up characters. Kids TV characters all with creepy smiles and santa hats. I could hear the hum of the fans from here. A chill ran down my spine and I wrapped my arms around myself, trying to keep warm.

"Can we go, please?" I muttered. The magic that I felt earlier was gone and now all I wanted to do was crawl into bed.

"How about we get some hot chocolate first to warm you up on the way home?" His eyes were searching my face, probably trying to figure out what I wouldn't let him see. But he didn't press me further. He simply waited for me to answer his question.

I sighed, trying to think of a reason not to. When I came up empty handed, I nodded. "Yeah, sure."

Eli led the way to a small coffee cart at the end of the street, a small line already forming. We stood in silence as we waited. Thankfully, within minutes, we were at the front of the line.

"Two hot chocolates, please," he asked the woman. She quickly poured the dark chocolatey liquid into two styrofoam cups as Eli fished a five dollar bill from his wallet. "Keep the change."

My hand grazed his as he handed me my cup, the warmth immediately rushing through my body. "Thanks," I whispered to him and we headed down the cleared sidewalk.

We walked most of the way in silence. I turned every corner as though it were second nature, focusing on my hot chocolate to keep from looking at Eli.

He cleared his throat as the house came into view. "You know, my sister used to always melt peanut butter into hot chocolate. It sounded so gross I never wanted to try it, but now I kind of miss it." He paused. "And her."

"I wish I had the chance to meet your sister, she sounds great, but I have to admit that combination sounds absolutely disgusting," I said with a chuckle.

"Yeah, well lucky she wasn't your sister then, right?" he snapped back at me. "You don't have to try any gross hot chocolate combinations."

"That's a bit harsh, don't you think?" I halted and waited for him to apologize, but it never came.

"I don't know," he said. "I can't figure you out."

"What? Can't figure me out? What about you and your cryptic comments?" I shook my head, feeling like my heart was being ripped in half. I finally remembered why I didn't get involved. Everyone hurt me eventually, it was inevitable.

"Yeah. I can't figure you out. One second you're kissing me and we're having a good time and the next second you freeze me out and I'm not allowed to hold your hand. Why won't you tell me what's going on, Lottie?"

His reply made my blood boil. If he couldn't see it, maybe he never would. "I don't know what you want me to say. There's nothing to say, actually. I think I'll take my own car to work tomorrow."

"Maybe that's a good idea. It'll give us both a little time to think and cool off." He unlocked the door and held it open for me to go inside. "I'll see you after work tomorrow?"

I nodded, even though I wasn't sure what I wanted and I got the feeling that he didn't either. It felt like we were just prolonging the pain. He made it perfectly clear that I wasn't going to stay here forever, this wasn't my family. So sooner or later I was going to leave.

I brushed past his shoulder and didn't wait for him before closing myself in the bedroom. As the door shut behind me, the tears finally fell. They cascaded down my cheeks in rapid fire. Sooner or later I was going to leave and I was starting to think that sooner was better. I had a choice to make. Take a bearable amount of pain now or stay and deal with the unbearable pain later.

There was a clear, logical winner.

I didn't get a wink of sleep. Even though I knew what I wanted to do, it didn't make it any easier. I must have went over my plan a hundred times and still, there was a voice in the back of my head that begged me to rethink things.

I sat on the edge of the bed as I heard Eli puttering around, getting ready for work. As I closed my eyes, I could picture him pouring himself a cup of coffee and smiling at me as he pulled a piece of toast from the toaster. Gosh, I was going to miss this. Miss him. But I just didn't belong here.

My family was somewhere out there and now it was time to go find them. Reaching toward the door knob, I pulled it open gently, but only a crack. As I peered through, Eli came into view and he walked toward the front door. He quickly disappeared from my line of sight and I bit down my lip to keep from crying all over again. This was it, the last time I'd ever see him.

I heard the door close behind him and the familiar rumble of his truck. He was gone.

Everything was so quiet, I felt like I had to tiptoe through the apartment. With my bag in hand, I slowly made my way into the kitchen. The plate from his toast was still sitting on the counter. I tidied up and took a piece of note paper from the drawer. I couldn't help the tears from filling my eyes as I wrote.

Eli,

Thank you for everything, but I have to finish what I started.

Goodbye,

Lottie

From my back pocket, I took out my earnings from the cafe. It would cover the part for my car and then some, but it put my stomach at ease knowing that after this, I didn't owe him anything.

I took one last look around as I backed toward the door and wiped away my tears. This was it, the ending that I'd been dreading. It left a bitter taste in my mouth as my heart longed for Eli to come barging back in and tell me to stay. Of course, that was nothing but a pipe dream.

Closing the door behind me, I muttered to myself, "Goodbye Eli."

CHAPTER 19

Cole Blackwood

I woke up in the morning to a silent house. As my eyelids fluttered open to the sound of my phone blasting the alarm, it suddenly dawned on me how comfortable everything had become with Lottie. I was used to her fumbling around my kitchen trying to make toast before work, even though Mom had offered to feed her at the diner more times than I could count.

The floor creaked when I stood up in front of the couch, and the wind whistled through the slightly ajar window. I slid the window firmly shut and locked it before making my way to the bathroom to get ready.

Should have put the coffee on first, I thought to myself as I turned on the water to brush my teeth. *Haven't had to do that since Lottie showed up.*

I shook my head and finished washing up before heading to the kitchen for my usual breakfast of toast and coffee. When the toast popped, I reached for the bread to put in another, but Lottie wasn't there to eat it. *It's amazing how quickly you fall into new routines when...* I didn't know if I was ready to even think it out loud.

I stared towards Lottie's door—I mean, my door. I wanted to go to her and explain my ridiculous behaviour the night before. In fact, I'd spent most of the night awake thinking about how I could make it up to her. But something had stopped me from walking to her door.

A small beep from my phone reminded me I had to leave to get to work. I rushed around the counter to grab my keys and wallet and then, without a backward glance, was out the door. I glanced over to the corner of the street, where I had parked Lottie's car after bringing it home yesterday. *At least she'll have a way to get to work.*

Then, I got into my cold truck and was on my way to work. Without Lottie for the first time in what felt like forever. The steering wheel was cold against my hand the whole time.

I was on my third oil change of the day when my phone started ringing.

"You gonna get that?" Joe called across the shop.

"Nah, I'm sure it's nothing." I dragged myself out from under the hood. "If it's really important they'll call back."

I didn't hear the non-committal sound Joe must have made as he went back to paperwork and invoices. With the amount of paperwork he was always doing, I wasn't sure I ever wanted to own a shop. But maybe the stability would be something... *No.*

"Cole!" Joe yelled across the shop only seconds later. "Your mother's on the phone and I do not get on her bad side so clean yourself up and get in here and talk to her, yeah?"

I wiped my hands on my rag and jogged across the shop, showing Joe my clean hands before picking the phone up off the desk. "Hey, Mom. What's up?"

"I'm just calling to check in on Lottie. I do expect my employees to tell me when they aren't going to be here on time, even if those employees are dating my son."

"We aren't dating, Mom," I started, and then it clicked. "Wait, Lottie isn't at the cafe?"

"No. Now why didn't you tell me she wasn't coming in."

"She was!" I protested, thinking back to our conversation from last night. "She said she'd take her own car today and... Oh no! I gotta go, Mom."

I didn't even speak to Joe as I raced out the door. Fumbling with the door of my truck, I finally managed to land my fully greasy self into the front seat and get the car in gear, racing off towards the diner and the path Lottie would have taken to get there.

Something is very wrong. Lottie would never show up late. She must have crashed.

My mind raced with so many worst case scenarios as my stomach turned itself into knots. I would never forgive myself if she got into an accident because of me.

Three complete circles through town to check every possible route between my house and the diner, and I'd seen no evidence of her or her car.

Where could you be, Lottie?

There was only one place she could be: at home. It made no sense that she would just drop everything and stop going to work, but it was the only thing that made sense. Maybe her car had broken down right at the house or something. I ignored the beeping of my phone, which was probably yet another text from my mother demanding I call her back after I unceremoniously hung up on her.

I must have had to stop at every red light in town on the way back to my house. *I'm sure she's fine,* I reasoned with myself. *I know I fixed her car and I double checked it had gas. Plus, she said she'd talk to me after work.* I also hadn't received any strange calls from people around town telling me Lottie was stuck in a snowbank or something, so she probably just slept in.

Which is very unlike her. But not impossible.

I rounded the last corner onto my street and noticed the distinct empty space where Lottie's car used to be parked. I was about to turn back around and head back to the shop, but something told me to go inside.

I came all the way here. Might as well check before I head back out to look for her.

I pulled my coveralls around my chest, attempting to prevent the cold from shooting daggers into my chest, but to no avail. Fumbling with my keys, I managed to get the door open before I completely lost feeling in my fingers.

"Lottie?" I called out, walking down the stairs. "Lottie are you here?"

I stopped at the bottom of the stairs, listening for any sign that she was in the bathroom or otherwise indisposed. Hearing nothing, I gingerly made my way down the hallway, past the empty bathroom to the open door of Lottie's—I mean my—bedroom.

"Lottie?" I called again before poking my head into the bedroom. The bed was made and the towel she must have used to shower that morning was hanging over the back of the chair.

So she didn't sleep in, I thought. *But since I'm here I might as well grab a coat and then call Mom and tell her Lottie left so she shouldn't be much longer.*

I opened the closet and noticed a suspicious hole on the shelf. Space I had cleared for Lottie the day after she arrived was now filled with nothing but air. *Had she just not put anything there this whole time?* I shrugged and pulled a jacket off the hanger, but a niggling feeling made me check under the bed. Her bag was gone, too. And her most prized possession in that stuffed animal.

The lump grew in my throat as my hand hovered above the handle of the top dresser drawer where I knew Lottie had been keeping her clothes. I wanted to open it. I wanted to know if she was really gone. But I also didn't want to believe it. She couldn't have left me without even saying goodbye.

"No, no, no!" I said out loud as I looked into the empty drawer of my dresser. *There has to be some other explanation. Maybe she's just upset about our fight and wants to move out of the room.*

I pulled my phone out of my pocket—thirteen new messages—and dialed the diner.

"Eli?" came my mother's frantic voice from the other end. "Eli where did you go?"

"I was just coming home to check on Lottie. I didn't see her car anywhere and she isn't here so she must be almost there. I'm sure she'll explain what happened when she arrives."

"Eli," she sighed. "That doesn't excuse..."

I didn't hear what she said next, because I was walking down my hallway to head back to work when the pile of crumpled bills on the counter caught my eye. *Why is there money on my counter?*

I wanted to believe it wasn't true, but the sinking feeling in my stomach told me I already knew why. Lottie was paying me back for the car. I'd really messed this up.

I can make it up to her tonight, though.

I was determined to put myself back together and return to work, but another piece of paper caught my eye. Sitting beside the money was a piece of paper that was too small to be her bill, so it had to be a note.

Maybe she wants to talk as much as I do. Maybe we'll go out and look at the stars and drink hot chocolate again.

The knot in my chest twisted tighter still as I came to rest in front of the note, clearly written in Lottie's hand. I barely had to glance at the note to realize that my worst fears were confirmed.

She's gone.

But I read it anyway. And then I read it again. And then I dissected everything that went wrong while my phone rang.

And rang.

And rang.

The next thing I knew, I was sitting on my kitchen floor clutching a note in my hand while my mother burst down the door like a SWAT team and rushed down the stairs.

"Eli, if you aren't dead, I'm going to kill you!" she shouted on her way down the stairs. "You scared me half to—"

The sight of me, tears streaming down my face, must have given her the wrong idea. "Oh, Eli. What happened?"

I shook my head, pulling in breaths that stabbed the back of my throat.

"Lottie. She's—" I handed her the note and she sank down beside me to read it.

"Oh, I'm so sorry, Cole," she whispered.

"I didn't even tell her. I should have told her. And now she's gone."

I let the tears stream down my face as my mother wrapped her arms around me and patted my back. The pain of Lottie's leaving tearing deep into my chest as the sobs wracked my body.

CHAPTER 20

Charlotte Sweet

My mind was racing a million miles a minute, but I just sat there, still. Frozen. Even though this was the decision I'd made, I wasn't sure it was the right one. I kept hearing Eli's voice in my head, trying to guide me in the right direction, but I shook it away. He was out of my life now and the thought made my body physically ache. Tears pooled in my eyes as I placed my hand on my chest. Small breaths filled my lungs as I tapped against my chest, counting my heart beats. I had to find a way to move forward.

This was my last chance at happiness. Less than fifty feet to the right. Only minutes away. It would have been an understatement to say that I was scared. Terrified, really. How was I supposed to do this? Meeting my family was everything I dreamed of, but was it worth the risk of putting myself out there again? There it was, Eli's voice was back. *Of course, it's worth it,* he'd say.

"Damn you," I muttered and wrapped my hands around the steering wheel so tight it made my knuckles turn a pale white. Moving on felt like it was impossible. In such a short amount of time I made a life, but it was what I did best. I was trained to leave my life behind and start over. I'd done it time and time again. Nothing was different now. I had to just keep telling myself that this was my way forward, everything else was in the past now.

Maybe it would all be okay. I'd get what I'd always wanted. It was out of character for me to be this hopeful, I never considered myself to be an optimist. I prided myself in seeing things from a glass half empty. Preparing myself for the worst, but I couldn't do that here.

If I left empty-handed, I went back to living in my car. No job, no place to live. No Eli. I couldn't walk away empty-handed this time, because it was all or nothing.

"You can do this," I muttered under my breath, over and over, but it didn't change how I felt. Completely, utterly, paralyzed. Still, I picked myself up and got out of my car. The cold air hit me like a slap to the face. Maybe I should have taken it as a sign and retreated right then, but I didn't. I looked left and right before jogging across the street, my hands stuffed in my warm pockets. "You can do this."

It was a house of dreams. The kind with a white picket fence that wrapped around the front lawn. Bright yellow gables sat against the white siding. I felt weird peering in the window as I walked past, but I couldn't help myself. The TV played in the living room, even though there was no one watching it. Everything looked so inviting. The Christmas tree that was decorated elegantly, the family pictures that sat on the mantle.

I gulped, realizing my mother had more children after having me. It was silly to think that because she gave me away she didn't want children. I didn't know why she decided to give me up for adoption. It was part of the reason why I was here. I wanted to know my family, my siblings. My hand trembled as I lifted it to the door. This was my last chance to turn back and forget about this whole silly notion. For some reason, I still couldn't find it within me to walk

I knocked. Not once, not twice, but three times before taking a step back. Time passed so slowly it was almost painful. All I could do was stand there and wait. The most painful part was I wasn't sure what I was waiting for. Of course, I knew I was waiting for my mother to answer the door, but then what? That was up to the fates and that made me shake in my boots.

Suddenly the door opened. A petite woman stood in the doorway, pulling her sleeves down over her bare hands as snow blew in. My mouth hung ajar as I stared at her, my mother. I found myself scanning her features, looking for similarities between us. Her hair was a dark mousy brown, but her eyes, her eyes were the same color as mine and she had the same dimples that formed when she smiled.

"How can I help you?" she asked when I didn't say anything. My hand tightened around the piece of paper that was in my pocket and slowly pulled it out. A copy of my birth certificate.

She quickly shook her head and began to close the door. "Whatever you're selling, we're not interested. Thank you."

"No um," I stumbled on my words, hoping she wouldn't shut the door on my face. "Sorry, I'm not here to sell anything."

"Oh?" she questioned as lines of confusion formed on her forehead.

I swallowed my fear and cleared my throat. "Are you Meredith Townsend?"

She nodded and furrowed her brows, opening the door back up just slightly. "Yes, I am. Do we know each other?"

"My name...it's Charlotte Sweet. I was born on July 9, 2001. I...you're my mother." My breath hitched as I spat out the truth. I tightened my hands into fists and dug my nails into the skin on my palms, afraid my whole body was about to give out and shake uncontrollably. Her eyes fell to the ground as she took several deep breaths. I could tell that I'd surprised her. Of course I had, she couldn't have guessed the daughter she gave up would be on her doorstep today.

Slowly, she stepped forward, her bare feet making imprints in the snow and closed the door. "A-are you alright? Is everything okay?" she said in a hushed voice, but her eyes didn't meet mine.

"Yeah, no...everything's fine." I blurted out.

"Then, what do you want? What are you doing here?" Maybe she didn't mean it to be harsh, but that was the way it came out. She finally looked up, her eyes glassy with tears.

I squeezed my eyes shut briefly and forced my bottom lip to stop quivering. "I just wanted to meet my mother, I thought maybe we could get to know each other. If that's something you would be up for. We could be a family."

"What about your family? Your adopted family."

I shook my head. She didn't know. "I...I was never adopted. I grew up in foster homes."

"I'm...so sorry, but I can't help you," she muttered under her breath as a tear slipped down her cheek. She quickly wiped it away as my heart sank into my stomach. She was an absolute stranger, but still, I got my hopes up that something good would come from this. I didn't understand what she was saying. I looked at the big house behind her and the life she had. Of course she could help me. "I can't help you. I gave you up. I was so young, I couldn't support you. You should go."

"But you can now, you have this house. You can support me now," I tried to reason. God, I didn't want to be wrong. She placed a hand on her chest and shook her head, holding back tears. Then, I understood. "Oh...you can, you just don't want to."

"I'm sorry, you should go. My husband...he doesn't know. You can't be here," she begged and stepped back into the house, about to push me out of her life forever, for a second time.

"So you're embarrassed of me?" my voice broke and I bit down on my lip. Now it was me who was trying my hardest not to cry. I knew that this could happen, that she could reject me all over again, but I didn't think it would really come to pass.

"No, please you have to understand..."

"I don't understand," I cut her off as tears slipped down my cheeks.

"Meredith, who's at the door?" a man called. Her husband, I assumed.

"No one, wrong house!" she replied, without hesitation before turning back to me. "Please, you should go."

The door clicked shut behind her as my whole world began to spin. Somehow I found my way to my car, stumbling across the road. Each breath I took caught in my chest and hiccup like noises erupted through my lips. This wasn't the way things were supposed to go. She was supposed to apologize for leaving me all those years ago and say how she'd do anything to make it up to me. That was what mothers were supposed to do, put their kids first. We were supposed to be a family.

My body hit the drivers side door as I sobbed, pathetically. The door handle gave way as I pulled and I flopped down into the seat. *I need to get out of here,* my brain screamed as I struggled to fit the key in the ignition. The endless stream of tears blurred my vision. My entire body felt hot as I thought about curling up in a ball and never showing my face again. The one person who was supposed to love me the most, didn't. The feeling of abandonment had been with me my whole life but now I knew for sure. She didn't want me. What was I supposed to do now?

It wasn't like I had an abundance of money burning a hole in my pocket. No, it was barely enough for a week's stay at a cheap motel. The leftover money from working at Jan's cafe.

I really didn't have anywhere else to go. No family and one too many burned bridges. There was no way that Eli would want me now. It was all my fault really that I had nowhere else to turn. All my fault.

How did I get here? How could I have been so stupid?

I couldn't catch a break. Why was I surprised? My life had been an endless string of letdowns. It wasn't about to turn around now. I floored the gas pedal and tried to wipe my tears away as they fell, but to no avail. My brain wouldn't let me escape the unease and doubt that I felt in my gut. There was no fairytale ending to my story. I was never going to get my happily ever after.

This was my downward spiral. My deep, dark, rock bottom. The moment where everything was coming full circle. I just had to find a way to accept that my life would never be the one I dreamed of. No matter how much it hurt my heart.

My hands tightened around the wheel as the sobs took over my body once again. I must have cried enough tears to last a lifetime, but still, there were more to come. The headlights that past were blurred by the liquid streaming down my face. Rays bouncing around the windshield.

I should have had the sense to pull over, find somewhere to spend the night, but something told me to keep going. Get as far away from here as possible.

Suddenly, the car skidded, like it was zooming across a slip and slide, but instead it was solid ice. My heart in my throat, I gripped the wheel tighter. Each attempt to regain control only made things worse. Life flashed before my eyes as the car began to spin. A complete three sixty.

This was it. This was the end. With my eyes clenched shut, I braced for impact, accepting my fate. As the car slid off the highway and sent me flying forward.

Goodbye Eli.

CHAPTER 21

Cole Blackwood

I spent the day Lottie left being treated like a child. My mother called my boss. *The embarrassment might never wear off.*

It took me several hours to convince my mother I didn't need to go stay with them for a couple days and was doing just fine. *I was not doing fine. And we both knew it.* But she had reluctantly left with the promise to return the next day after work for dinner. I spent the night curled up on the couch, not really sleeping. But I couldn't bring myself to go to my own bed. I couldn't look at the gaping hole she left in my closet. And my life.

The next morning I dragged myself around the house getting ready for work. It was impossible not to think about her. I splashed water on my puffy eyes and dried it with a towel that smelled like Lottie's shampoo. I made myself toast for breakfast and remembered our peanut butter and jelly candlelit dinner. I got into my truck and noticed her discarded coffee cup in my cup holder.

I couldn't even listen to the radio without thinking of her dancing to everything and anything that played. I switched to a local news station and quietly made my way to work. Lottie's leaving rested heavily in the air. Everything reminded me of her.

"What are you doing here?" Joe asked me when I finally made my way into the shop. "I thought I told you to take a couple days at home."

"I don't need a couple days," I lied. "Plus, I want to save my days for Christmas. My sister's bringing her kids and they are ... extremely energetic."

Joe chuckled but his smile didn't reach his eyes. The stern look reminded me, as everything else did, that Lottie had left me. Just picked up and left. *Just like she said she would. I shouldn't have expected any different.*

"Plus, you have a couple two man jobs today, right? Couldn't have you breaking your back trying to lift a car or something, Superman."

"Lift a car?" He raised an eyebrow and pointed to the service jack currently holding up the rear end of Mrs. Sanderson's SUV.

"Joke, old man!" I teased, doing everything I could to mask the gaping hole that grew inside of me.

We worked in silence for the next couple hours, only speaking of work topics. I left for lunch and sat alone in my car eating a sandwich I made out of whatever my mom had brought me the night before. It tasted like ham. My hand hovered over my cell.

I could just call her and see if she found them? I reasoned with myself. *Maybe just say I'm sorry for how I treated her. I hate that I left it like that. I hate that I caused her pain. . . that all sounds so tacky and fake.*

I opened the contacts and scrolled to Lottie's name. The smiling picture of her the night we got back from skating stared back at me, the smile reaching her eyes. *How could I deny her that happiness she so desperately deserves? Who am I to stop her from finding her mom.? From having a family?*

I could practically hear my father's voice in my head. "Son," he would say, "are you doing this for her? Or are you doing it so you can feel better?" Then he would go on a rant about apologies being for those we have hurt. And that hurting people more isn't worth it if it's only to assuage our own guilt.

"I'd be doing it for her," I thought aloud. "I want her to know I love ... I love her."

No, the truth on my shoulder spoke to me. *You want her to come back.*

I sighed and slumped forward onto the steering wheel. I don't know how long I sat there grappling with my decision. I only know that by the time my phone rang and I looked at the time, I was very late for work. "Boss Man" flashed across my screen as the cheery tune filled my car.

❄❄❄

By the time work was over, Joe's frown was tattooed on his face and my mother was calling me asking if I wanted to go there or if she would come to me.

I groaned into my hands and turned the ignition in my truck before sending a quick text to my mother. ***I'll come over once I'm done my laundry.*** It was a lie, but I knew she would object to my plan. And I knew she would never say no to cleanliness.

When I got home, I noticed Mr. and Mrs. Wilson staring out their window. Almost certainly at the request of my mother. So I waved and smiled, putting an extra bounce in my step as I walked into the house.

My arms shook as I got out of my work clothes, showered, and put on some dark jeans and a tee-shirt.

I stared at the phone on the counter. Sitting there. Tempting me.

I shouldn't call her. She knows my number and if she wanted to call, she would.

But what if she's thinking the same about me? How awful would I feel if I miss this just because I'm being stubborn?

How awful will you look whining about her leaving you when all she wants to do is find her mother?

Before I could talk myself out of it, I pressed down on Lottie's name and listened as the phone dialed and connected.

And rang. I could imagine her ringtone filling the kitchen of a cozy home as she cut apples up for a pie her mom was making.

I almost hung up. My finger hovered millimeters from the red end call button when a voice I didn't recognize picked up the phone.

"Hello?"

"Um. Hi, sorry. I must have the wrong number," I managed to stutter out. *Had she changed her number so soon? She must really not want to talk to me.* I could feel the tears stinging the back of my eyelids as I blinked and took the phone away from my ears.

"Are you looking for Charlotte? Who is this?" the woman asked. *Of course. Her mom.* I breathed a sharp sigh and nodded.

"Um, yes I am. Nice to meet you. I'm Cole Blackwood." I held my breath, preparing myself for the drop I would feel if she didn't want to speak to me. Truthfully, nothing could have prepared me.

"We were about to call you. Charlotte had you listed as an emergency contact in her phone. I'm sorry to have to tell you this, but she's been in an accident. She's here at ..."

The nurse or doctor kept talking. My whole head felt like someone had submerged it in a pool filled with bees. My ears filled with a strange buzzing noise and my eyes struggled to focus. It was only when a tear dropped onto my cheek that I realized I was crying.

"No," I whispered into the phone. "It can't be."

"I'm so sorry, Mr. Blackwood, but that's all I can tell you over the phone."

"Wait," I said, suddenly realizing I was speaking to a nurse and not Lottie. "Why did you need an emergency contact? What happened?"

"Mr. Blackwood, as I explained, I really cannot tell you more on the phone—"

"Let me talk to Lottie." The knot in my stomach tightened as the nurse said the words I dreaded.

"I'm sorry, Mr. Blackwood, but you can't speak to her. She's sleeping now. We will call you the moment she wakes up."

"Wakes up? When will that be?"

"Do you have someone who can drive you down here?"

I nodded again. "Yes. Yeah, I do."

Something glued me to the couch. Though I willed my arms to pick up the phone and call someone so I could get to Lottie, they did not comply. She was in surgery. She'd been in an accident.

What kind of accident? Would she even want to see me when I got there?

"There's no way I could leave her alone," I said, grabbing my keys and running up the stairs. "I have to go to her."

And I would have driven myself there, too, if I knew where there was. But I somehow failed to pay attention to that part. So I was stuck sitting in my truck dialing Lottie's number over and over until someone picked it up.

"Mr. Blackwood?" the voice from earlier sighed.

"Yes. Hello. I... I called earlier and you told me I could come see her but I don't remember where you said you were." I heaved a deep sigh and waited as she told me the name of the hospital (St. Something's) and the town it was in. I couldn't think clearly long enough to say anything of use, so when she hung up I called my mom.

"Cole!" my mother scolded when she picked up the phone. "You said you would be here half an hour ago."

"It's Lottie," I said without greeting. "She's been in an accident and she's at a hospital. She couldn't talk to me and I don't know what's wrong and..." I could feel my grasp on logic and calm slipping away as my body became a heated tense fire pit and the breaths poked needles into my chest.

"Where are you?" she asked, her jacket zipping and the keys jangling. "I'll be there as soon as I can."

"Home," I said simply. "Can you drive me?"

"Don't move. I'll be right there."

I'm pretty sure she had hung up the phone but I whispered, "thanks" anyway.

My head was spinning and my fingers were numb the whole way to the hospital. It's only about an hour and a half drive, but the fact that my mother wasn't filling it with educational radio or questions about my life was oddly unnerving.

Something is very wrong here.

Mom pulled the car up to the hospital entrance to let me out. "Do you want me to come in with you? I can park the car first if you want."

"No. I can do it alone." I pushed the door open. "I'll send you a text when I figure out what's going on and where we are. Okay?"

I didn't wait to see her nod, slamming the door behind me and racing into the hospital and up to the third floor at the direction of the stunned woman at the information desk.

"I'm looking for Lottie," I gasped to the first nurse I saw on the third floor. "I mean, Charlotte Sweet."

"Mr. Blackwood?" The woman at the desk looked up from her paperwork. "Are you Cole Blackwood?"

I nodded.

"Right this way. I'll take you to speak to the doctor."

Why can't I speak to Lottie? Is she...?

My mind was rushing through all of the worst case scenarios when the door opened in front of me and the doctor stood up to shake my hand.

"Cole. Please take a seat."

I crossed the room in less than three strides and sat down in the bright blue chair the doctor had indicated. Lottie was nowhere to be seen.

"So how is Lottie?" I asked him when he did not speak. "When can I see her?"

"She's just resting now and we've had to give her some pretty heavy medication so she might not be awake for a while yet, but we expect she will make a full recovery." He motioned that I should follow him as he led me out the door and into the hallway.

"With any accident this serious, there are several things to watch for in the next few hours. Once she wakes up, I'd like to discuss her injuries and treatment options with both of you. Do you have any questions for me right now?"

I shook my head. I'm sure I had hundreds of questions for him but my mind was coming up empty. All I could think about was Lottie.

"All right. Then I'll let you go in and sit with her. If she needs anything, there's a nurse call button on the side of the bed."

"Thank you, Doctor," I said, my hand already pushing in the door. As soon as it opened far enough to reveal Lottie's frail form lying in a hospital bed, I rushed across the room as quietly as I could.

"Lottie?" I asked, kneeling beside her bed and holding her hand in mind. "Lottie if you can hear me, it's Eli. I'm here."

She didn't respond, the only sound a shrill beeping from the machine beside her indicating her breathing and heartbeat.

I kissed her hand and rested it back on the bed. Kissing her forehead, I whispered the words I'd so desperately wanted to say since the morning I woke up alone. "I'm sorry, Lottie. And I love you."

The beep of the machine was the only sound that greeted my apology, so I pulled up another uncomfortable bright blue chair beside her bed and took her hand back in mine. *Please wake up, Lottie. I'm here.*

CHAPTER 22

Charlotte Sweet

Light burned through my eyelids as I fell back down to earth. The dream land had been so appealing. It was like floating on feathers. Warm, soft feathers. I wanted to stay there forever, even though it left a bad taste in my dry mouth. The taste of straight alcohol. Slowly I became aware of my body. My arms and legs were covered by a soft blanket that almost seemed weighted. So much so that it made it hard to move.

There was a tingling sensation in my fingertips as I realized there was a hand holding mine and tightly. A slow beeping filled my ears, becoming louder with each passing second. It made my brain pound in my skull until I forced my eyes open.

This wasn't a familiar place, but I immediately knew where I was. I knew just by the smell of antiseptic that filled my nose. My eyes trailed down my body, squinting through the blurry haze. A hospital gown loosely covered me, yet the fabric still made me want to scratch every inch of my body. Or maybe that was due to the medication that was slipping into my vein through the IV.

A boy sat next to me, leaning back in his chair with his eyes closed. I didn't have to see his features to know who it was. Eli. His name echoing in my head sent butterflies dancing in my stomach. Tears filled my eyes as I thought about the last time I'd seen him and the note I'd left. I couldn't help but think that maybe he was here to let me know how much I'd hurt him. To yell and get back at me for what I'd done.

I deserved to be yelled at. I deserved whatever he was about to say to me.

"Eli," I tried to say, but it came out cracked and raspy. Still, his eyes fluttered open. Those beautiful brown eyes that pierced into my soul. God, how I missed him. The tears streamed down my cheeks. *I'm such a bitch. How could I have hurt this beautiful man?*

"Hey," he muttered under his breath, a small smile on his face, but it quickly shifted to panic. "Are you alright? Are you in pain?" He stood and hovered over me, waiting impatiently for me to answer.

I cleared my throat and went to pull my hand to my face to wipe away the tears. Pain shot through my shoulder as my arm caught on the sling. "Sore, but I'm okay." My chest rose and fell as my palm became sweaty in his grasp. His expression relaxed and we quickly fell into silence, the past looming. It was my fault we were in this position, so I had to say something. Right? It was just so easy to get lost in his eyes and forget everything. "You're here... I didn't think you'd come."

"Of course I did," he said, but his teeth pulled at his bottom lip as though he was holding back what he truly wanted to say.

"Why?"

"Why?" he said, exasperatedly. "Seriously?" His voice raised, but he quickly composed himself. We were in a hospital, after all. He whispered through clenched teeth, "I care about you, Lottie. We had a fight, that doesn't mean I don't stop caring. Unlike you, I don't run away from my problems." I expected him to be angry, but I still wasn't prepared for this. I tore my eyes away from him as lips quivered. He folded his arms across his chest and sighed. "I'm sorry."

"It's okay, I deserved that," I muttered, but still I didn't meet his gaze. "I'm the one who should be sorry, Eli."

"Why? I fixed your car and you left, just like you said you would. You don't owe me anything," he said. *But then why do I feel like I do?* I bit my tongue. If that was how he truly felt, then why was he here? He obviously didn't feel the same way about me as I did about him. There was no hope for us, no hope for me. "Lottie, I'm glad you're okay though."

I knew what he meant. I survived a car accident. But I was far from okay. My car was totalled and now I truly had nothing. No family, no home, no prospects. I had nowhere to go from here. But sure, I was alive.

"What is it? What's that face?" he wondered out loud. I stayed silent. Telling him wouldn't have helped anything. It would have just made him feel sorry for me.

"Nothing, I'm not making a face," I lied, but he saw right through me.

"You're lying, Lottie. What happened? Is it about the car wreck or is it something else? Did you find your birth mother?" I still couldn't wrap my mind around how he did it. In such a short amount of time, he seemed to know me better than anyone else. *Damn, you.* I pursed my lips together and tried to hold in my tears. "Fine, don't tell me," he huffed.

He was frustrated with me, I would have been too, but little did he know, I just didn't know how to tell him. No one wanted me, not even my own mother. I couldn't say it out loud without feeling my voice fail me and tears spring to my eyes. Rock bottom wasn't exactly attractive.

"What happened? Why are you acting like we don't know each other, like these past few weeks have meant nothing?" he asked genuinely. He seemed like he really wanted to know.

I gulped and forced my voice to leave the safety of my throat. "What did they mean, Eli? Tell me, because I don't know." My tears committed a treachery, slipping down my cheeks.

His hand left mine and clapped against his thigh. "What do you mean you don't know? You were there too."

"I mean, my car broke down and you helped me which was very kind of you. It was a nice vacation from the real world, but that's all it was. A vacation. We both knew I had to go back to my life. Which sucks because it's not like I have much to go back to. I don't have a family to go back to, I have..." I quickly wiped my tears away and corrected myself. "Had my car. It's time to go back to reality, Eli. My reality."

He chuckled, shaking his head at me. "Do you really think that low of me? Lottie, you could have stayed."

"Why? I would just be prolonging the inevitable. So no thank you, that's not what I want."

"Then what do you want?" he demanded, sitting back down in the chair to look me in the eyes. "What do you want?"

"God, Eli. I just want to be happy! But I just wrecked my car, after my own mother told me that she didn't want me because she was embarrassed of my existence. Is that what you wanted to hear?" My hand flew up over my mouth to hide the sob that escaped my lips.

"No," Eli muttered under his breath, just as distraught by the news as I was. Slowly, his fingers intertwined with mine once again. "Shit, I'm so sorry, Lottie. I wanted it to work out, you know I did."

Silence loomed as neither of us knew what to say now. We were at an impasse. I knew deep down that it was me who had to apologize. Eli didn't do anything wrong. This was all on me.

"I'm sorry that I didn't say goodbye. I got scared and I bailed. You're right, I ran away," I told him, finally admitting it to myself, but even in that moment I was still scared.

"It's okay, Lottie."

"It's not." I shook my head. "But okay."

"And hey, you don't have nothing. You have me," he said, trying to lighten the mood as he squeezed my hand lightly. "And I'm not going anywhere."

"You say that now, but..."

"Lottie, I promise," he swore and I believed him. He scooted closer to me. "I-"

"Ah, there are my babies," Jan cried as she rushed into the room with both arms open wide. Her eyes locked with mine. "How are you feeling dear?"

"Alright," I muttered as my tongue grazed my dry lips. There wasn't a world where she didn't know what I did to Eli. Hell, I also left her high and dry at the cafe when she had been nothing but kind to me. If I were her, I would have been mad. An apology plagued my brain, but the words just wouldn't escape my mouth. It was like I was frozen, looking into her deep down eyes trying to figure out how she felt. But all I found was kindness.

"I spoke with the doctor and once you sign the discharge papers you are free to leave," she said, sitting down in the corner of the room and clasped her hands in her lap.

My heart plummeted into my stomach. *Free to leave.* It sent shivers down my spine. My gaze flickered up to meet Eli's.

"You'll come home with us, okay?" he suggested, before turning to his mom. "Right, Mom?"

"Yeah, of course." She smiled. "You're always welcome, hun."

❄❄❄

With each pothole my brain thumped against my skull, making me wince. I could feel Eli's eyes on me as he glanced in the rear view mirror. I was told that I was very lucky, I only ended up with a minor concussion and a dislocated shoulder. It could have been much worse according to the firemen that arrived first on scene. Just a few feet from where my car landed was a bridge that covered a ravine. Still, it felt like the worst case scenario. I didn't have the money for a new car. If I were dead, I wouldn't have to worry about the cost of my funeral.

I mentally smacked myself for thinking such awful things. Eli's voice echoed in my head, *you're alive, you should be grateful. I know I am.* Even though he hadn't actually said those words, it brought a smile to my face.

As we turned into the subdivision, I got the feeling of deja vu. Just weeks ago, I was coming here for the first time after Eli rescued me in the snow. Cold with doubt swirling around in the pit of my stomach, unsure how I was going to go forward. So much had happened in such a short amount of time, yet I still felt the exact same way.

Life had taught me one thing, there was no one I could rely on but myself. As much as I wanted to rely on Eli, I couldn't because the voice in my head kept saying, *what if?* What if it didn't work out a week from now, or a year from now? I'd be back in the same place, but what other option did I have?

He pulled into the driveway and quickly came to my door, helping me out of the car. With an arm around my waist, he guided me toward his house. My hand shook in his and I hoped that he would think it was because I was hurt, not because I was scared out of my mind.

Jan clasped her hands together as we walked inside, warming herself up. "Let's get you set up in the guest room, I think you'll be more comfortable there where you can rest. Are you hungry or do you want something to drink? Or is there anything else you need?"

"I got it, Mom," Eli answered.

"Alright, baby," she said and squeezed his shoulder, before walking into the kitchen.

Eli carefully slid my coat off my one good arm and slipped his hand back in mine. We made our way silently to the bedroom. With so many thoughts swirling around in my head, you'd think I would have been able to come up with something to say, but I didn't know where to start. Saying something usually just made things worse. I sat down on the edge of the bed as Eli opened the closet and pulled out a new set of pillow cases and an extra blanket.

"You can stay here as long as you want, Lottie," Eli began as he sat down beside me. "Look, I know it couldn't have been easy, what happened with your birth mother, but blood doesn't make family. I've gotten to know you and you're so special Lottie. To me, to my family. My mom, she adores you as you can probably tell and uh- I,"

"You what?" I asked when he paused.

"I love you, Lottie," he let out, exasperatedly. "I love you. There I said it."

He took my breath away, literally and figuratively. I was left without an ounce of air left in my lungs. Why did I find it so hard to believe? Eli loved me. How could he love *me?* My eyes filled with tears. I wanted nothing more than to hear him say those words, yet it sent fear to my heart.

"What's wrong now?"

"We can be friends, we should be friends. Just friends," I cried, even though the very same words were on the tip of my tongue.

He shook his head. "You don't feel the same way..."

"No...yes...I mean, what if it doesn't work out, Eli? What if we get our hearts broken? You're all I have right now, and that scares the shit out of me. I'd have nowhere to go if... We can be friends. Things can stay the same, right?" I spoke through the sobs that made my head pound.

"W-we could." He nodded as he scooted closer to me, wrapping an arm around my waist. "But, Lottie, I..."

"You don't want to just be friends," I deducted.

"Do you love me? Because if you do, I say we give it a shot. I know you're scared, but you know I'd never just throw you out on the streets right? And you can work at the cafe, or find a job somewhere else in town and save up some money. We could make a plan. We could make it work, because I love you. I can promise you that," he said, his gaze never leaving mine, not even for a second. "Do you love me?"

The fear still sat in the pit of my stomach, but as my lips parted, I knew in my heart that this was what I wanted. "I love you, Eli."

CHAPTER 23

Cole Blackwood

She loves me.

Warmth flooded my skin at the confirmation of what every part of me had longed to be true since I'd met her. Her shoulders relaxed into my chest when I wrapped my arms around her and pulled her into me, kissing the top of her head. I was really glad she couldn't see what was surely a goofy grin spreading across my face.

The ticking on the clock and the slow movement of Lottie's shoulders kept the time as we sat on the edge of the bed.

"Lottie?"

"Hmm?" came her groggy reply.

"I was just going to ask..." I paused, waiting for her response. "Are you tired? Do you want to go to sleep?"

She turned her cheek into my chest and nodded. "Mmm hmm."

"Okay, let's get you under the covers."

Lottie pushed herself up off the bed and wobbled slightly, sitting back down. "I think the room is spinning a little."

"The doctor mentioned that might happen for a couple days. Do you want me to help you?"

Her nod was small as she let me put her arm around my shoulder and pull her upright.

"Can you wait a second? I feel like I might be sick." Lottie's eyes were closed and her free hand pressed into her temples.

All I wanted to do was make it better. But there was nothing I could do except what I already was. "Are you alright if I hold you with just one arm? I can get the blankets and pillows set up enough for you to sleep, I think."

"I think so. Try it. I just want to sleep."

It was hard work holding Lottie upright while moving the pillows and blankets into place. I tried not to jostle her too much but her couple well-masked winces made it abundantly clear I was failing. *Typical Lottie, not telling me something was hurting her.*

"Okay. I think that's good enough. Let's get you into bed shall we?"

She didn't make a sound as I lowered her into the bed and guided her head toward the pillow. Once she was safely laying down, I lifted her legs and pulled the blanket up to cover her.

"That good? You comfortable?"

"Mm hmm."

"Okay. I'll be back to check on you in a couple hours."

Though her eyes were closed I could tell she was glaring at me.

"Doctor's orders, remember?"

When she didn't answer, I reached over and turned out the light next to the bed. "Goodnight, Lottie," I whispered, kissing her forehead.

"Eli?" she asked, reaching her hand out to stop me.

"Yes?"

"Stay with me."

It wasn't a question. It wasn't even a statement. It was a plea. A plea from the core of Lottie's being: to have someone who would stay with her.

"Of course," I whispered, tears threatening to spill out onto my face. With Lottie now safely in bed for the night, I was finally allowing myself to feel what I hadn't been able to all day. The gravity of everything she had been through in the last day, crashed over me like a tsunami as I crawled into bed beside her and put my hand into hers.

And I meant it. I would stay with her. Forever if she'd let me.

But a small part of me, or rather a large part, still wondered if she would have me. *She loves you, Eli. Trust it.*

I don't remember how long I laid there, with Lottie's gentle breaths counting the time. I only remember my phone alarm waking me every couple hours to wake Lottie. And each time she woke, the knot in my chest loosened a little bit. Each time she swatted at me to let her sleep but sat up and sipped her water, I felt a little more sure of what tomorrow would bring. When I finally woke her for the last time at eight o'clock in the morning, it almost seemed like the last few days hadn't happened.

But they had. And I'd have to deal with that. *But first, breakfast!*

❄❄❄

It turned out our conversation was delayed by a lot more than breakfast as my mother decided to make an impromptu visit to check up on Lottie. Or so she said. If I know her at all, it was also to check up on me. But she had brought supper, so it wasn't all bad.

It was only Lottie's dramatic yawns around seven that caused my mother to even think about leaving.

"I'm so sorry, Jan. I guess this concussion makes me more tired than usual. Thanks so much for dinner." Lottie was her usual charming self.

"Oh, no dear I'm sorry. I should have thought of that. I'll just put away these dishes and let you get some sleep. I'm just so glad you're okay." My mother's eyes glanced away from Lottie for a moment to meet mine. I nodded, hoping to give her the confirmation she needed to believe that I was going to be okay.

"Really, though. Thanks for dinner. We really appreciate it." The 'we' just slipped out of my mouth like the most natural thing in the world, but Lottie looked at her hands and a pink blush crept into her cheeks.

"You know what, Mom. How about I finish putting the dishes away? You've done more than enough for us and I'm sure I can handle it. You taught me well." I might have thrown that last part on to butter her up. Lottie was looking both embarrassed and exhausted and there were some things I really had to get off my chest before we went to sleep and I completely lost my nerve. Again.

"All right. If you say so." Her eyes were calculating as she looked between the two of us, but in the end she dried her hands off with the towel, kissed me on the cheek, and put on her coat to leave. "I hope you feel better soon, Lottie. I'll come check up on you tomorrow if you want. Just give me a call or text okay?"

We both nodded our agreement before she found her way up the stairs and the door clicked shut behind her.

"She really does love you," I said, putting the three plates away into the cabinet. "I mean, she does like to dote on people, but she likes you."

"Yeah." Lottie's voice was quiet and she was staring at the fireplace.

This doesn't look like a good time. Maybe she really is tired. I reasoned with myself, the towel tightening around my hands as I wrung it.

"Lottie? Are you okay to stay up a little longer? There's something I wanted to talk to you about."

I held my breath.

"Yeah." Her hand patted the couch beside her and I obliged, filling the spot and wrapping my arms around her. She settled into my side and took a deep breath.

"I'm guessing you want to talk about what happened."

I nodded, and then realized she couldn't see me. "Yes. But first, I want to talk about what happened before you left, if you don't mind. The rest can wait until tomorrow if you're tired." The sweat was already beading on my forehead. I had to get this out. *She deserves to know.*

My breath shook as I took a deep breath to steady myself. "This is going to sound like a really weak excuse. I want you to know I'm not trying to excuse my actions. I am truly sorry for how I treated you that night. I shouldn't have snapped at you and I should have let you make the call of telling me when you were ready. That part, I want you to know, I don't excuse. I'm sorry."

I paused for another deep breath, and when Lottie didn't say anything I launched into the rest before I could lose the nerve.

"Well, when I was little, I had a sort of strained relationship with my sister. She's almost ten years older than me so I was always trying and failing to get her attention. Back then, she would do everything she could to shake her kid brother. She was a teenager and I guess it wasn't cool to have a seven year old hanging around. Some of the only times she'd let me spend time with her was when she'd take me skating and we'd get hot chocolate on the way home. She'd put peanut butter in it and always ask me if I wanted some."

A chuckle escaped my lips thinking about her beaming face when I finally agreed to try it. "Well, finally one day I agreed to try it and it was actually pretty good. And it became our thing. It was the way we reminded ourselves we were a team, even when nothing else seemed like we were. And our relationship is a lot better now, obviously, but that memory is special to me. And I wanted to share it with you again. Here. In a place where you could understand what it meant."

My God, I'm not making any sense.

Everything I just said seemed so trivial at that moment. She'd been to see her birth mother, maybe, and gotten into an accident that gave her a concussion. She had no family to speak of and I was here blabbering on about how hard it was to get along with my sister because we were ten years apart.

The word 'sorry' was already on the tip of my tongue when Lottie's soft voice broke the silence. "That sounds like it was special. I'm sorry I didn't listen. It honestly wasn't your fault, I was just upset because I thought once my car was done, that was it, and I took it out on you. I'm sorry. Sometimes I get in my own head about stuff and get a little too defensive. I should have listened, too."

The silence filled the room again, and my tongue was probably bruised from stopping me saying anything.

"So, if you want, I'll accept your apology. But you have to accept mine, too."

I couldn't help the small chuckle that escaped my lips. "Of course."

Lottie turned to look at me. "Good." Her eyes brightened with her smile. "And there's some things I want to tell you, too. But I really am tired. Do you think you could get tomorrow off work so I can explain it to you?"

How could I say no to that?

CHAPTER 24

Charlotte Sweet

Eli's promise was still playing on repeat in my head, *"We could make it work, because I love you. I can promise you that."* And even though I knew that he meant it, I couldn't shake the feeling in the pit of my stomach that it would all fall apart. I was just hoping that with time, it would fade. Maybe telling Eli what happened with my birth mother would help the doubt wash away. The truth was healing after all, or so I was told. As I stared up at the ceiling, I was working myself up to telling Eli everything, no matter the consequences. The fact that he was hugging me tight made it easier, his arm draped around my waist.

I felt him snuggle in closer, if that was even possible and lay a gentle kiss on my cheek. "Morning," he said, his voice full of early morning rasp. The deep tone sent butterflies dancing around in my stomach. "How are you feeling?"

"Better," I muttered, feeling a smile pull at my lips. I turned toward him slightly and my eyes locked with his. "Thanks to you."

"You give me too much credit." His low chuckle made his chest vibrate against me and a shiver ran down my spine as he ran a hand through my hair.

My teeth grazed my lip as I felt a pang of guilt. "I wouldn't be here if it wasn't for you. I'd probably be in some shelter or in a tent out in the cold. You don't give *yourself* enough credit, Eli and I love you for it."

A big smile appeared on his face and as his gaze fell, his eyelashes brushed over my cheek. "I love you too," he muttered under his breath.

I gulped. There was no better time to tell him the truth about why I left and what happened with my mom. Sure, he knew some, but he deserved to know it all. He needed to know what he was getting himself into. I was like a snowball of doubt, rolling downhill only to crash at the bottom. "So uh, Eli, you know how I said yesterday there was something I wanted to tell you..."

"Yeah," he said, meeting my eyes once again as his hand stroked my arm, gently. A silent, but welcomed reassurance.

"Well, uh-"

Just as I began, the ringing of the phone cut me off. "Sorry, I'll be right back," he jumped out of bed and rushed into the kitchen for the phone. The breath that I had been holding inside my lungs, slowly escaped, although the tension in my shoulders didn't seem to want to leave. Not until Eli knew everything.

I pulled myself upright and leaned back against the headboard. Even though Eli was on the phone, I could still hear Jan's voice on the other end, laughing about something her son had said. Time passed slowly as I waited for him to come back, even if it was just mere minutes. His footsteps drawing near brought a smile back on my face. He stopped in the doorway and leaned against the frame, crossing his arms and his feet.

"I know we were in the middle of something, but I have a surprise for you. If you're up for it, of course," he said, calmly, but by the smile on his face I could tell he was really excited about whatever it was that he had in store for me. Just holding it in to see what I thought first.

A nervous giggle escaped my lips. "You know what I think of surprises," I teased, but I knew I wanted to experience whatever he was so excited for. "But yeah, let's do it."

He threw himself down on the bed, a big goofy smile on his face and planted a kiss on my lips. "Okay, get dressed into something warm, then we can get going. It's nothing strenuous I promise."

"And we can talk later?"

"Yeah, of course. We can even talk when we're there if you want." He hopped up and rummaged through his closet, pulling out something to wear. "I'll let you get dressed. Holler if you need anything."

"Okay."

❄ ❄ ❄

It was only a short car ride to wherever it was that Eli was taking me, but even as we got close I still didn't know what the big surprise was. All that was in sight was hills of snow, vast empty fields, and an endless amount of evergreen trees. I was bursting at the seams, the anticipation slowly building up in my mind. No matter how much I pleaded, Eli kept his mouth shut, although he couldn't help but smile with one hand on the steering wheel and the other resting on my thigh.

"Close your eyes," he said, suddenly.

I turned and gaped at him. This didn't seem like a normal request, at least not one that I'd experienced before, but Eli's expression seemed strangely normal. "Close my eyes?"

"Yes, close your eyes! You don't want to ruin the surprise, do you?" he asked, just as we rounded the final corner. Even though I didn't quite get how the two were connected, I listened and closed my eyes.

I held my hands up in surrender. "Happy?"

"Yes, very," he said genuinely. I entwined our fingers and sat back, trying not to let my heart leap out of my chest. My toes tapped anxiously against the floor of his truck. Eli let out a low chuckle that rumbled throughout the cab and I felt his thumb begin to draw circles on the back of my hand. "Don't worry, it's a good surprise. I promise."

"I'm just excited to see what you have planned and you know I'm impatient."

"Well, we're here, so no more waiting." Right on cue the car slowly came to a stop and he put the car in park. My eyes flickered open, but Eli was quick to cover them back up with his hands. "Not yet. I'll tell you when you can open 'em."

"Okay," I groaned.

He took his hands away and I immediately felt the warmth of his body disappear. Cold air blew through the cab of the truck as his door opened and then he shut it without saying a word. I sat in the unwavering silence, my hands pressed underneath my legs to stop from shaking. I tried to convince myself it was because of the cold, but a brief wave of worry washed over me. *What if he's left me here?* A voice in my head answered, *you mean like you left him?*

I jumped, startled when the door opened. "Sorry, didn't mean to scare you. You can open your eyes now."

"It's okay," I muttered as my eyes opened and readjusted to the light. Eli held out a hand to me, helping me from his truck. I almost missed the sleigh off to the right, with a gorgeous black and white horse strapped to the front and a burly man dressed up like Santa Claus. My eyes searched the surroundings. It seemed to be a horse farm. A barn was in the distance and the woods lined a small field. "What are we doing?" I asked, still confused.

"What do you think, silly? We're going on a sleigh ride," he said, matter of factly, stepping to the side so I could get a full view of the sleigh.

My eyebrows raised instantaneously. "Seriously?"

"Yeah." He nudged my shoulder lightly and placed a hand on the small of my back. "After you."

"What? How?" I questioned, feeling my whole body begin to turn to mush as I stepped onto the sleigh and sat down. It was like I had been transported into a romantic comedy movie once again. Another magical moment that Eli had somehow figured out how to give me. I didn't even know this was something I wanted, until I was sitting in the sleigh with the snow glistening in the sunlight.

Eli sat down beside me and rubbed his hand over the back of his neck. "I uh- actually had it organized before you...left. My mom reminded me about it."

"I'm sorry." Guilt radiated throughout me as I saw the hurt in his eyes. How he found it within him to take me back after everything I'd done, I still didn't know. Never in a thousand years could I repay him for his kindness and knowing I'd hurt him made every bone in my body ache. "This is amazing, Eli."

"It's okay, it's all behind us."

The sleigh jolted forward and the horse began trotting toward a trail at the side of the property. Trees caved around the open path and created a tunnel of light. Snow clung to the branches and fashioned a gorgeous winter wonderland. I latched onto Eli's arm, giggling softly to cover my embarrassment, but my eyes were drifting through the luxurious snowy scenery.

"Actually, Eli, it's what I wanted to talk to you about. I feel like I owe you an explanation," I said.

"No-"

"Please, just let me get this out." I forced myself to look him in the eye as he nodded in agreement. A shaky breath entered my lungs as my heart began to pound in my chest. "I'm so sorry, Eli, for leaving without saying goodbye. After everything you've done for me, it was wrong and I knew it, even while it was happening. There's no excuse for what I did, but I really didn't want to hurt you, Eli. I really didn't. For so long, I've just been running away and I got scared, because I fell in love with you. I couldn't see how it could ever work out, because I was leaving to find my birth mom and I didn't have anything to give you in return. And it's not your fault, it's mine for letting my past get the best of me, but you were talking about what a perfect last night it was and I didn't want it to end. Then we got in that fight and I started to feel like I was intruded on your family. So, I guess I ruined it. I just left and I'm so sorry. You deserve so much better than that. And I know you say it's in the past, but Eli, I'll spend every minute of every day trying to make it up to you."

"I'm sorry too, Lottie. It's not all your fault. I should have done, or said something to make you know that you were wanted here. That *I* wanted you here," he said and turned slightly to face me. He came closer and closer, until I could feel his breath against my cheek. I thought he was going to kiss me, but instead he whispered in my ear. "I want you here."

My heart lurched and tears pooled in my eyes. Those words meant everything to me. *Everything.* "I'm really happy I'm here."

"Me too," he muttered and finally kissed my lips. I felt him smile as I leaned into him and as we broke apart, I rested my head onto his shoulder.

"Now, let's enjoy the ride," I told him as the sleigh continued to glide down the path and we traveled deeper into our own little Christmas paradise.

CHAPTER 25

Cole Blackwood

She had seemed so earnest when we spoke, but the truth was everything bad that had happened in the past, as far as I was concerned, was completely behind us. But there was one thing that was left undone and with the help of my entire family, I was hoping to fix the problem of Lottie not feeling like she belonged. So we spent the rest of the 23rd shopping for a new outfit for Lottie. I convinced my mom to help, so she insisted Lottie needed to have a new Christmas dress, but wouldn't tell her why. I knew Lottie enough to know she would have resisted any gifts from me, but she was powerless against my mother. We had that in common.

So when three in the afternoon rolled around on Christmas Eve, I was left standing in the living room waiting for Lottie to change into a dress I had yet to see at the request of my mother. All I knew was it was going to fit into the family picture.

"Lottie, we are going to be late for supper at this pace. The kids might actually kidnap you if you delay their festivities."

"I'm coming!" she called from the room. "Just putting on the finishing touches."

At my mother's request, I had a very Christmasy red tie with white and silver snowflakes on it. *At least it's not a tacky sweater like last year.*

I reached down to slide my gloves out of the overnight bag I had packed the night before and zipped it up. Then I slid the handle over the small suitcase I had made Lottie pack despite her protests.

"Lottie? I'm going to take the bags to the car and I'll meet you out there okay?"

"No need. I'll come with you," she said as she appeared around the corner of the hallway, sliding a small earring into her left ear and twirling around once. Her confidence wavered only for a moment when she asked, "Do I look okay?"

My jaw slackened and I couldn't help but look at her. The long sleeved red dress was lacy almost and it was tight to all of her. "You are drop dead gorgeous," I answered honestly. "Wow."

"Okay, that's enough flattery for one day, Mr. Blackwood. Let's get to your parents' house already." Before I could even move again, she had picked up the bags and carried them, along with her shiny black shoe, up the stairs. "You coming or are you just going to stay here with your jaw on the floor all day?" she teased when she reached the top and slid her shoes on.

"Yeah, I'm coming." I bounded up the stairs two at a time and slid my gloves on, locking the door behind us while Lottie threw the bags into the back of the truck. She really was remarkably strong for someone that small.

As usual, the drive was filled with Lottie dancing to whatever music was on. In this case, some kind of strange blues country Christmas mix I personally couldn't stand, but Lottie made everything interesting. So by the time I put the truck in park at my parents house, I was also dancing along to what was left of a beat in the terrible Christmas music.

I couldn't help but watch Lottie's hair fall into her face while she danced to the last notes. Before I could even make the conscious choice to get out of the car, Ben and Sarah came running out of my parents' house screaming for me.

"Are those your sister's kids?" Lottie asked, her face aglow with a smile I hadn't seen leave her face since this morning.

"Yes. They are going to ask you to help them put out the reindeer food. Just go with it."

Her laugh rang through the car and I had to catch myself from staring. Everything about her was so inexplicably carefree. She reminded me, in a way, of a child on Christmas morning. The magic of Christmas was still as fresh for her as it was for Ben and Sarah. I should have thought of that.

When I came to my senses, Lottie's door was already open, her hands reaching down to give hugs to my niece and nephew. "Hi," she said. "I'm Lottie. You must be Gabe and Resa." They dissolved into a fit of laughter and Lottie brought her hand to her mouth in mock surprise.

"No, silly." Sarah giggled. "I'm Sarah. He's Ben. I'm his sister."

"Oh. Well, it's very nice to meet you Sarah. And you too, Ben."

My sister must have heard their interaction because she laughed and waved at me from the doorway. I got out of the truck and waved back, walking around to Lottie's door and scooping up Ben. "Hey little guy. Shouldn't we be wearing a coat outside."

"Guncle Lie, no." He shook his head violently and crossed his little arms across his chest. "Sweater."

My sister's face was buried in her hands, but I couldn't help but laugh. "Well, a sweater is also very warm. What are you doing out here?"

Sarah answered instead. "Mom said we could put out the reindeer food as soon as Uncle Eli came. And you are here, so let's go! Let's go!" The force with which she tugged my arm was far beyond her almost four years.

"Come on, Lottie!" she added as we pulled away from the truck. "If we don't feed the reindeer Santa might not make it!"

Sarah dragged us both along until we reached the pail on the porch. "Mom, Uncle Eli is here!" She didn't even wait to hear Resa's answer before picking up the bucket. Ben squirmed out of my grasp and fought her over the handle of the pail, spilling some in the process.

"Okay, Lottie, let's go! We have to put it out so the reindeers can eat. They will find us faster and Santa will be happier, so we'll get presents. Come on!" Her little hand tugged Lottie's and they were off, Sarah explaining the whole process to Lottie as she went, and correcting Lottie's every mistake.

When they finally came back to us, all three of them were almost in tears from laughter. My heart warmed to see Lottie so carefree with them. It was part of what I loved about her.

"What is so funny, Sarah?" my sister asked.

"Ben fell down and Lottie tried to catch him, but he went spinning and now he's a snowman! Look!"

Ben toddled out from behind Lottie, covered in snow and licking some off his hands. "Fall! Fall snow!"

"I'm so sorry," Lottie said through laughter. "I really did try to catch him."

"Don't worry about it, hun. We've seen far worse before. You'll get used to him eventually."

I heard Lottie whisper, "eventually," under her breath when Resa turned and headed into the house, but I didn't say anything. It was nice to see her enjoying herself and I couldn't wait to share more of our Christmas traditions with her. If I was being completely honest, I couldn't wait to make new Christmas traditions with her. A thought both terrifying and exhilarating at the same time.

❄❄❄

Lottie spent the lead up to dinner in the kitchen with my sister and mother. Apparently, I was not allowed because someone needed to help those wild children wrap their presents. So needless to say when we sat down at the table, I was keen to sit far away from the mashed potato cannon and his sister. My mother's seating plan mercifully obliged as Lottie and I found ourselves at the far end of the table, meaning that when dinner was over, we managed to keep our clothes relatively free of food.

"Shall we get out the Christmas Crackers?" my mother asked the room, which murmured back its yesses to her. "Lottie, would you like to help me get them from the other room and pass them out?"

Another one of my mother's plans to make Lottie feel at home, probably. I couldn't help but wonder what those two talked about when I wasn't around.

Lottie's hair bounced with every step she took, following my mom out of the room and coming back in with an arm full of Christmas crackers which she handed out, one by one, to everyone around the table by name.

"There's too many!" she said when she arrived at our seats with three crackers still in her hands. "One for you. One for me. One for your mom."

"Two for you!" Sarah declared from the other end of the table. "Lottie can be first AND last!"

"Can't argue with that." I smiled and took a green cracker from Lottie's hands. "Leave one for Mom and pop yours open."

She set down her purple and gold Christmas crackers before placing a red polka dot one in front of my mother's chair. Her hands twisted at the hem of her dress as she always did when she was nervous.

"Together?" I asked, picking up the gold one and holding it out to her.

"Okay." She slid into her chair and copied how I was holding the cracker.

"One, two, three ..." I began.

"Pop!" Ben yelled as I said, "Pull," and pulled on the cracker as Lottie held the other side tightly.

"Pop! Pop!" Ben giggled and clapped as the confetti flew out of the cracker and into Lottie's face. I picked up the little top that had fallen out and unfolded the pink crown, placing it on Lottie's head.

"There should be a joke in here somewhere, but I can't find it."

"It's okay," she said. "I'm a princess so..."

We went around the table until everyone had a crown and Lottie had a second one placed upon her head, giving her a very clown like appearance. Fortunately, Lottie had come to the rescue with some hair pins when Ben's crown was too big for his head. He wasn't quite as keen on a necklace as his sister had been.

As Lottie was dragged off to help my mom, the kids made hot chocolate for everyone, and the other's cleared the table. Resa pulled me into the hallway.

"What?" I asked when she just stared at me.

"What?" she asked, raising her left eyebrow. "You seriously asking me that right now? Look at you?"

I looked down and saw nothing weird about my outfit or anything. "Look at me what? It's you that's covered in Ben's potatoes."

I don't think I've ever seen her roll her eyes that dramatically.

"You know full well I mean Lottie. Look at how you are with her. And she has PJs in the pile so I assume Mom knows."

"Yes, Mom knows about Lottie," I sighed. "Thanks for checking in, *Mom*." I rolled my eyes, hoping to get that dramatic stubborn child effect, but when I looked back at Resa she was peering past me into the kitchen.

"I like her," she said finally. "I just want to know why I wasn't told. I mean, do you know how hard it is to find a present around here this close to Christmas? I had to visit Mr. Goldblum at home and actually beg him to sell me something for Lottie."

She playfully smacked the back of my head like she always did when I was a kid.

"Sorry!" I rubbed the spot she had hit, even though it didn't really hurt. "There's been a lot going on."

"You can tell me all about it later," she said.

Dropped that a lot easier than I expected. I would find out why when Lottie's voice rang out through the hallway. "Everyone to the living room for hot chocolate and the movie! We have no time to waste!"

We were soon settled in on every surface in the living room, just like we always did. We nestled into the corners of couches and squished two people on a chair meant for one. Lottie sat almost on top of me, while I sat on a cushion on the ground. The short cartoon version of How the Grinch Stole Christmas played on the television as my hot chocolate grew cold on the side table. My arms were more focused on holding Lottie close than anything else.

"You didn't drink your hot chocolate," she remarked when the movie was over.

"I'll get it later." I was trying to be cool, but she could see right through me. *Time to divert.*

"Isn't it far past time for some little ones to go to bed?" I loudly asked the room. "Does that mean we should do our one last Christmas Eve tradition?"

"Yes! Yes! Yes!" Sarah practically bounced with excitement while Lottie looked at me quizzically and Ben tried to keep his eyes open from his father's lap.

"Why don't we hand them out, Sarah?" I reached out my hand for her and she sprang across the room like a gymnast. "I'll help you read and you can pass out the presents."

Everyone knew what the presents were. Even Sarah probably knew. But no one said anything as we made our way around the room handing out the wrapped presents to everyone in turn. They were probably all hoping to see Lottie's face at the surprise.

And she didn't disappoint. When she ripped the wrapping paper off her pair of new pajamas, she smiled and looked around the room. "Whoever this is from... thank you."

"It's from us, Lottie," my dad unexpectedly spoke. My mom usually would have answered for the both of them. "We get a new set of matching pajamas every year, so the whole family matches on Christmas morning."

My mom cut him off. "You don't have to wear them if you don't want to, dear. But we just wanted to get them for you."

"No, I love them." The tears that threatened the edge of her eyes proved just how much that was true.

"Well," my Dad said, clapping his hands together. "I think it's time for us all to head upstairs to our bedrooms for a little reading and bed. Wouldn't want Santa to be delayed because we're all still downstairs."

We all wished each other goodnight and then I led Lottie up the stairs to my childhood room. Of course, my mother had dutifully set up the bed and a cot for us. Once we had each taken our turn getting ready for bed and changing into our pajamas, we closed the door and crawled under the covers of my old room's double bed. The light from the table lamps mixed with the twinkling Christmas lights through the window as we cuddled together. The last thing I remember before closing my eyes was Lottie placing a gentle kiss on my temple and whispering, "Thank you."

"No," I whispered back. "Thank you."

CHAPTER 26

Charlotte Sweet

That night, sleep had never come so easy. The second I closed my eyes, I was out like a light and I fell asleep with no worries playing through my head. No doubts. Just the serenity of pure happiness. The spirit of Christmas created a warmth that radiated throughout me, warming a place inside of me that I thought would stay cold for eternity. Even if this was just temporary, I was going to let myself want it. I told myself that this was a good thing that I couldn't ruin. At least not this time around.

Fool me once shame on you, fool me twice shame on me. And Eli was no fool, neither was his mother.

After years in foster care, I thought I'd finally mastered the art of sleeping through anything. But I was wrong. Two kids bursting through the bedroom door and hopping into the bed shook me from my slumber. Excited screams echoed in my ears.

"Wake up! Wake up!" A little girl's voice pipped. "Santa came!"

Her screams were followed by a toddler's hands pressing against my cheeks. "Presents! Presents!"

My eyes flickered open as Eli pulled his niece and nephew down on the bed, immediately jumping into uncle mode. "What? Santa came?" he said, surprised. Putting on a show. Sarah and Ben giggled loudly, only making Eli's smile grow. It was easy to see how much he loved his family. Unconditional love.

I sat up and leaned against the headboard, watching as Eli set the kids down on their feet. Both tugged at his sleeves, pulling him out the door. "Come on, Uncle Eli! It's time for presents!"

"Okay, I'm right behind you!" he said, but instead of following them down the stairs he turned back to me. His smile grew as he neared, leaning over the bed to give me a quick peck on the lips. "Merry Christmas, Lottie."

"Merry Christmas," I quickly echoed, still in awe. After I slipped out of bed, I pulled a sweater over my head. "Come on, we don't want to keep them waiting."

"Oh trust me, they've probably already started ripping into their stockings. In this family Christmas morning is a free-for-all," he chuckled and intertwined our fingers, guiding me slowly toward the staircase.

As we made our way down, the Christmas tree slowly came into view and I had to stop my jaw from falling to the floor. Christmas music played quietly in the background as Resa hugged her mother and father. Presents overflowed out from underneath the tree and right in front was a pink Barbie dream house with a bow on top. I remembered when I was younger tearing a picture of one out of the wish list catalog to include in my letter to Santa. Though I quickly learned that Santa was a mere myth, I wanted Sarah and Ben to hold onto the magic of Christmas for as long as possible.

I leaned into Eli's shoulder and watched as Sarah saw the gift that every girl dreamed up. Her eyes lit up and a gasp slipped through her lips. "Just what I wanted!" she said and rushed toward her big present.

"We have to open our presents together, but then you can look at your dream house," Resa guided her daughter over to the couch where her stocking sat, stuffed full with goodies.

"Yours is over here beside mine," Eli whispered, tickling my ear. I followed his gaze to the sofa and saw the knit red stocking with my name stitched into the fabric.

"This is for me?" I muttered under my breath, letting myself fall back into Eli. With both hands fixed on my shoulders, he guided me to the sofa and sat me down.

"All for you," he said, though it sounded more like a promise. He sat down beside me and his knee slowly fell against mine. Although my eyes were busy taking in my surroundings. The room felt warm, full of excitement and love. Voices chimed in each and every direction, making it so I could barely keep up with all of the different conversations. Everyone slowly began to settle in, sitting beside their respective stocking.

Jan clinked her spoon against her tea cup, scooped up her bounding grandson and held him on her lap as she spoke. "I'm so thankful to have you all here for another year. Christmas wouldn't be the same without my family." Her eyes landed on me, her gaze lingering before continuing. "Which little munchkin wants to hand out the gifts?" she asked as she tickled Ben's sides.

"Me! Me!" Sarah jumped out of her seat and dove toward the Christmas tree.

"Remember, give one to everyone," Jan reminded.

I sat back and nestled into Eli's side, ready to watch everyone open their presents when Sarah placed a small gift in my lap. This day was proving to be full of surprises. I really didn't expect there to be anything under the tree for me. Maybe it was from years of experience, or maybe because of everything I'd put Eli through. We'd only known each other for a few weeks afterall.

"This one's from me," Eli said with a big smile on his face.

I gulped, immediately feeling guilty. He meant so much to be, but yet again, I had nothing to give him in return. "But I didn't get you anything," I mumbled as I frowned.

"You don't need to get me anything. You're here that's all that matters," he said with a wink. "It's just something small anyway. I saw it and thought of you."

He placed a small kiss on my forehead and nudged my shoulder, urging me to open it. I let out a sigh and fiddled with the tape on the wrapping paper, being ever so careful not to rip it apart.

Eli chuckled lowly, the vibration traveling through me. "You don't have to be so gentle."

"Okay, if you say so."

I tore through the paper and revealed Eli's gift. He was right, it was just something small, but little did he know it meant the world to me. A small ceramic bear hung on a strand of red ribbon. It was a Christmas tree ornament that meant so much more.

"It's Herbert," we said in unison as tears pooled in my eyes.

Not only was it a symbol from my childhood, it was also a gift from Eli. I wanted to throw myself into his arms and burst out crying, but I remained composed and tried to express my gratitude with words in light of his family being in the room. "It's perfect, thank you."

"You're very welcome."

"Keep the presents coming, Sarah." Jan's laughter broke me from my thoughts and Eli quickly caught up, opening up a new pair of oven mitts from his mom.

"Thank you, Mom. I needed a new pair," he said.

I chuckled, remembering the nacho making fiasko. "He's been using a dish towel."

"Cole!" Jan remarked, ashtoned. "In the spirit of Christmas, I'm going to forget about that."

"That one's for Lottie, be careful with it please," Resa instructed her daughter and I quickly looked to the oddly shaped object in Sarah's hands. A gift from Eli was one thing, but Resa too? I didn't know what I did to deserve such kindness and to be included in their family Christmas. And that was the thing, I was sure I'd done nothing to deserve it.

"You didn't need to get me anything."

Resa shook her head. "Oh hush, everyone deserves presents on Christmas."

"Here you go," Sarah muttered, handing the gift to me sheepishly. I probably wouldn't have even bothered to wrap it if it were me, just stuffed it in a bag with some tissue paper. Resa must have been a very patient person. She probably needed to be to handle Ben.

"Thank you," I cooed and waited for everyone else to have a present in their lap before I began to open it.

At first I couldn't tell what was inside. It wasn't until the wrapping paper fell to the floor that I realized it was a wood carving of a reindeer all painted as though it would be pulling Santa's sleigh. I could have sworn I even saw a twinkle of magic in its eye.

My heart felt light, full of love. For so long I'd been searching for a family to call my own, and I honestly thought, here with the Blackwood's, I found it. I looked between all of the smiling faces and lastly at Resa, who was awaiting my reaction. "It's beautiful. Thank you so much."

"I'm so glad you like it. Reindeer have a special place in this family."

"I love it," I corrected.

"Every year my mom would give us all a new reindeer decoration. They do the hard work pulling Santa's sleigh after all. That's why the house is filled with reindeers," Eli explained.

Resa quickly added, "Now you can start your own collection."

"That's perfect. I'll cherish it forever. Thank you, again." I hugged the carving tight to my chest before setting it down carefully on the coffee table.

"Can I open my dream house now?" Sarah begged her mother, but Jan answered for her.

"How about you hand out one more round of presents and then Lottie will take over for you? There's one last present for her under the tree." She pointed to a small present in the far left corner and Sarah quickly scurried over to it, giving it a light shake. When it made no noise, she frowned and set it in my hands.

This one, unlike the others, had a tag. It read, *To Lottie, Love Jan.*

For some reason, my heart began to pound in my chest at the thought of seeing what was inside the nicely wrapped present. I couldn't even begin to guess. I knew no matter what it was, that I would like it, but once again I had nothing to give her in return. She wouldn't have wanted anything, but I still felt the need to repay her for all of her kindness.

"Don't wait for the other's, open it up!" Jan urged me.

I nodded and took a deep breath before ripping the cute winter themed wrapping paper. Fabric was neatly folded inside, but I could just make out my name embroidered in the top left corner. With shaky hands, I took it in my hands and revealed a cooking apron.

Simply the fact that it had my name on it was overwhelming. It was truly mine and she had gone through the effort to let me know that.

"Before you say anything, this gift comes with a...proposal, if you will," she began and laid a hand gently on my knee. "I'd like for you to come and work for me full time in the dinner, if you want to of course. It would just be minimum wage and the hours can be long, but we have a lot of time. What do you say?"

I was stunned, to say the least. She had nothing to gain from hiring me, well other than having an extra employee and I was so grateful. My life was about to change, I could feel it. Yet this time, I wasn't scared. Just excited for what was to come in the new year.

I nodded, quickly, waiting for my voice to catch up. "I would love to work for you. That would be amazing. I can't thank you enough, Jan."

She pulled me into a hug and whispered, "Merry Christmas, Lottie."

I wiped away the tears that escaped and sat back. Eli's arm wrapped around my shoulder and I snuggled into his side, my heart feeling whole as I watched the Blackwood family unwrap the rest of their presents. The more I didn't want the magic of Christmas morning to end, the more it flew by. It was a feeling I wished that I could bottle and keep forever. However, I had a feeling that in this family, there was plenty more where that came from.

Once all of the presents were opened and the contents from the stockings were splayed out on the furniture, Jan was off to prepare a fabulous brunch. Resa hurried her two children to the entryway and with the help of her husband, got them ready to play in the snow. Anything to entertain them for a while until the brunch was ready. Her words, not mine.

I got up off the couch and wrapped my arms around Eli's waist, or as far as I could at least. "Hey, thank you for this. This is the best Christmas ever."

He looked down at me, a goofy smile on his face. "You're welcome."

Resa peeked her head around the corner and giggled. "Someone's standing under the mistletoe."

Both Eli and I looked up and sure enough, right above our heads was mistletoe. "Well, I guess that means we have to kiss."

"Oh, do we?" I said, teasingly, but narrowed the distance anyway. I didn't need to be asked twice.

Our lips touched and just like the very first time, it sent a tingling feeling throughout my body. It was the kind of kiss that filled my soul with happiness and just from the way his hand caressed my cheek, I knew that he loved me. Sometimes, actions spoke louder than words.

Eli broke the kiss, but held me close and tickled my cheek with his lips. "Merry Christmas, Lottie."

"Merry Christmas, Eli."

THE END

Don't miss out!

Visit the website below and you can sign up to receive emails whenever Alice Fox publishes a new book. There's no charge and no obligation.

https://books2read.com/r/B-A-FXZMB-DTZHF

BOOKS 2 READ

Connecting independent readers to independent writers.

Also by Alice Fox

More Than Roommates: An Enemies To Lovers Romance
His Bossy Obsession: A Billionaire Boss Romance
The Boss's Big Secret: A Billionaire Boss Romance
Falling for the Bosshole: A Billionaire Boss Office Romance
Taming the Bosshole: A Billionaire Boss Office Romance
Last Flight To Stardom: Enemies to Lovers Romance
Love In Full Bloom: Small Town Romance
Raindrops Over Texas: Small Town Cowboy Romance
Say Yes To The Boss: A Billionaire Boss Office Romance
Crushin' on Fame: A Billionaire Boss Romance
Dirty, Rich, Boss: A Billionaire Boss Office Romance
Queen of Hearts: A Dark Mafia Romance
Lost & Found: Small Town Romance
How Not to Fall For The Boss: A Billionaire Boss Romance
Irresistibly Bossy Collection: A Billionaire Boss Romance Collection, 3 Books In One
Behind Office Doors: A Billionaire Boss Romance
Finding Home: A Christmas Sweet Romance

Milton Keynes UK
Ingram Content Group UK Ltd.
UKHW030949261124
451585UK00001B/118